FOX RIDGE

THE SECRET

BONNIE MARLEWSKI-PROBERT

Whitehall Publishing
PO Box 548
Yellville, AR 72687

http://Whitehallpublishing.com

https://www.facebook.com/bonnie.marlewskiprobert

https://twitter.com/BonnieMarlewski

info@Whitehallpublishing.com

REVIEWS

"I loved all of the characters!! Katherine seems like a familiar person to me. Having spent time around horse folks, she reminds me of several women I have known throughout our horse showing years- extremely independent, somewhat stubborn and highly competitive- but with a heart of gold and very giving...

I liked the way that Katherine's "secret" unfolded. It kept my attention and I honestly did not know what her secret could be-until it finally was unveiled." Diane K. Swafford, Charlotte MI, lifetime horse lover.

TABLE OF CONTENTS

AUTHOR BIOGRAPHY

Bonnie Marlewski-Probert is an international bestselling author. Her background includes 20+ years as a professional teacher, trainer, speaker and author for the horse industry. She is the author of more than 26 books and has published more than 1000 magazine articles around the world in a wide variety of markets both in and outside the horse world.

She started writing as a professional while still working fulltime in the horse industry, both as a syndicated columnist and freelance magazine writer before she signed her first book publishing deal.

She founded Whitehall Publishing in the early 90s and has published the works of hundreds of authors from around the globe in both fiction and non-fiction, including everything from biographies, children's books, religious works, WWII fiction, how-to books, fund raising works for non-profit organizations, medical works and more. Her firm has published award winning books and has produced dozens of bestselling authors in the process.

Bonnie splits her time now between running Whitehall Publishing, working with animal-related non-profits (Therapeutic Riding Centers, Dog/Cat Shelters) and on her free time, writing contemporary romance.

If you are a writer looking for a way to publish your work while maintaining creative and financial control, visit http://whitehallpublishing.com.

CHAPTER 1: MORNING TRAINING

W ickedly talented on horseback, Katherine McMahon, the petite, red headed owner of Fox Ridge Equestrian Center was a study in contrast. On the one hand, she'd worked hard to make sure her customers felt like they were part of a family, but Katherine had no family of her own. Warm, outgoing and cheerful on the outside, while at the same time riddled with shame, fear and guilt on the inside. She demonstrated a keen, focused interest in the lives of her clients which allowed her to hide her own sorted past in plain sight. All of the things Katherine McMahon created for her customers were precisely the things she desperately longed for in her own life, but knew she could never have as long as she remained haunted by her past. Yes, Katherine McMahon was a contradiction.

Ж

Mercedes Benzz, the large chestnut gelding exploded over the five-foot oxer, his hooves pounding the ground in harmony to the driving beat of the Clapton/Santana guitar riffs blaring throughout the expansive indoor riding arena early that Monday morning. The fall air was crisp as Katherine powered her mount over the course of six fences, making it look easy. At 16.3hh, the gelding made Katherine look like a child on his back. Notwithstanding, she was a grown-ass woman of 30 years, her 5'4" petite frame often led people to initially doubt her ability to handle the massive equines in her charge, that is, until they saw her ride.

Benzz, as Katherine called him lovingly, was her personal show horse and the only tie to her old life in New York. It was their success in the show ring in North Carolina that *put her on the map,* six years ago to the day, when she opened Fox Ridge Equestrian Center.

After schooling the gelding over the course, Katherine pulled the small fob out of the pocket of her fitted black breeches and clicked it to turn off the stereo that sat secured to the rail against the wall.

"Jimmy, I'm going to finish up with some flat work. I'll ride Jackson next. Go ahead and tack him up now, I'll work him over the same course but let's drop the height down to three feet for him and then let's work the bay. We'll finish the morning on low fences with the green mare," she called out from the opposite end of the large arena.

"Ok Katherine, I'll have them ready for you." Jimmy Weston, her cheerful 25-year-old barn manager headed for the stall at the end of the aisle where Jackson, the large grey gelding was stabled. Jackson's owners named their horse after General Boregard Jackson of the Confederate Army. His gray color reminded them of the uniforms worn by the Confederates during the civil war. *In the South, Katherine learned quickly, history still mattered.*

The pair trained horses early each morning, long before the barn officially opened at 9 am so Katherine could indulge in her two favorite vices; training jumpers and loud music, both of which put her in a zen-like state of mind. The duo worked together effortlessly, Jimmy handling things on the ground and Katherine handling business in the saddle.

The barn was a magical place early in the morning, especially in the fall when the trees were ablaze with color and the air was crisp. The sunlight glinting off the rafters, the sounds of birds fluttering through the expansive covered arena looking for pieces of grain left behind after the morning feed. The smell of sweet feed and alfalfa hay, mixed with the smell of Horse were all intoxicating to Katherine McMahon. Recognized as a Master when it came to training horses and riders, she only wished she was half as gifted when it came to her personal life. It wasn't that men weren't interested in her, it was her fear that they would get too close that kept her isolated and admittedly, more and more often, lonely.

She hit the fob one more time to turn on the stereo, gathered up her reins before pressing Benzz into a soft posting trot on the left hand track. She cut a smart figure in her black breeches, knee-high hunt boots and today, a pink polo shirt. The duo would spend the next 10 minutes working on extensions in both directions before swapping mounts.

Even though Katherine's focus was on turning out great jumping horses, Fox Ridge boasted both Western and Dressage instructors too. Her goal was to create a facility that focused on embracing all styles of riding and all breeds of horse while providing enough income streams to keep her staff employed in what could sometimes be a tough industry. One of Katherine's greatest strengths was making sure she always had plenty of options. That skill was honed out of necessity.

While she and Jimmy went from horse to horse as they did each morning, today was different for Katherine. Her mind was clouded with concerns that she couldn't ignore. The Hunter/Jumper facility in Canada wanted her decision on their job offer and she had no idea what to do. *I don't know if I can leave Fox Ridge,* she thought. *Alberta Canada is far enough away that there would be almost no chance anyone could find out about my past. Being Head Trainer would allow me to ride all day and not have the responsibilities or the headaches of owning and managing a facility and I would get a steady paycheck.* She learned the hard way that only her staff received steady paychecks, while the barn owner got paid after everyone else got theirs and then, only if there was anything left after all the surprise bills were paid, like roof repairs or broken water lines. *It could be a fresh start and maybe then I could finally risk having a personal life,* she pondered as she rode her final horse for the morning.

Since that horrible night, six years ago when she lost her husband, Katherine moved to North Carolina and away from everything she knew and loved in New York. The only human tie to her past was her best friend

Sharon McMaster (now Pinter) whom she'd known since they were both kids riding ponies in upstate New York. Sharon still lived there and was happily married to Roger Pinter, a successful businessman climbing the proverbial corporate ladder. The couple celebrated their first baby girl, Pamela, the year before. In six years, however, Sharon had never visited Fox Ridge and Katherine had yet to meet Sharon's daughter in person, although they had met during screen shares online. It was all at Katherine's insistence because she couldn't risk her *past life* meeting her *present life* and while Sharon didn't like it, she of all people respected the need to keep Katherine's secret. After all, she was there that night.

CHAPTER 2: DOCTOR BAKER

"Bob, good to see you. How's Mary?" Katherine gave him a warm hug.

"She's chomping at the bit for me to retire and travel in our RV," he said with a smile. Dr. Robert (Bob) Baker was a tall, distinguished older gentleman. His thick white hair made him stand out in a crowd. Bob had been Katherine's barn vet since the beginning.

"Mary is being very selfish. Doesn't she know I need you to be my vet forever? What in the world am I going to do without you?" Katherine asked truthfully with a smile on her face as they headed into her office to get the list of horses that needed attention.

"Don't worry, I'm selling the practice to a younger vet named Brandon Stafford. He's a really nice guy and he knows his stuff."

"Well, I have a bit of news as well," Katherine whispered, closing the office door behind them.

"What's that?"

"I'll only keep you a minute. I was offered a big job at a farm in Canada a few days ago," she whispered.

"No kidding? Are you going to take it?"

"I don't know. My heart is here but the offer's really good. It's a Head Trainer post with the opportunity to move up to management in the years

9

to come and you know I'm not getting any younger, so I need to start thinking about the future."

Bob laughed, "I have boots older than you! In fact, the pair I have on right now were probably bought when you were in grade school."

"As much as I love having my own barn, there is something to be said for not having the responsibility for every detail, from lightbulbs to roof repairs and the thousands of other details I have to deal with. If I were head trainer, I could focus all my attention on turning out the best horses without the distractions that come with owning the barn."

"I know everyone would miss you if you left," he said sincerely.

"Thanks for that. I hope you won't mention the job offer to anyone except Mary, of course, until I make up my mind."

"No worries, other than my Mary, my lips are sealed. So, when do you have to decide?"

"I asked them to give me a few weeks. Well, we'd better get to it," Katherine grabbed the list from her desk and headed toward the main barn isle.

"Right, so who are we working on today?"

"I have a boarder's horse, Beau, that's got a pretty nasty cut. It might need a few stitches and two school horses that just need annual shots. Who do you want to start with?"

"Let's handle the cut first and finish up on the shots."

Katherine called out, "Jimmy, would you bring Beau up for me please?"

"Sure."

The two spoke while they waited for the horse to arrive. "Bob, I really am going to miss you when you retire. Nobody can take your place! How many vets would've stayed in the barn with me all night babysitting that sick foal last year? You're one in a million."

"It was my pleasure to babysit with you that night. You fed me well and it wasn't that uncomfortable snoozing on hay bales. You know, if I were younger and single, that could have been quite an exciting night for everyone."

"Oh no you didn't just say that!" Katherine laughed. "What in the world would Mary think if she heard you talking like that? Besides, no matter how irresistible you may be, I'm a woman on a mission and I don't have time for men in my life. So, when are you officially leaving us?"

"I'll shadow Brandon for the next month and then in late November, I'm going to officially retire so we can travel around the country in our RV and see the kids. Our first stop is Thanksgiving at my daughter's house up north. You know Mary has been after me for years to slow down and smell the roses. I guess it's time to do that before I'm too old." Just then, Jimmy entered the aisle with a large grey gelding.

"Kate, can this old man share a bit of wisdom with you?" Bob asked while watching the big gray move past them.

"Sure, I'm all ears and by the way, I don't think of you as an old man."

"Look, I'm in my late 60's now and realizing I might have more years behind me than in front of me. I just have one regret in this life, that I didn't focus more of my time on loving the people who mattered to me most. I was so focused on building the practice that I didn't spend enough time with my family. When those years with your loved ones are gone you can't get them back," he said sincerely, taking her by the hand and squeezing it gently. "Kate, I want you to fall in love with someone wonderful and have lots of babies and create a family of your own."

Katherine knew Bob was sincere and he wanted only the best for her. He couldn't have known that she desperately wanted the same things, but knew they could never be hers. Not now. Not ever. "Bob, Mary already scooped up the man of my dreams! If I can't have you, I don't want any other man." They both laughed.

Despite her laughter, he could see that she was saddened by what he'd said to her, although he couldn't have known why. In an attempt to lighten the mood, Bob headed down the aisle, "So, Jimmy, is this Beau?" Bob casually studied the horse's body and every muscle in motion as only a veterinarian can.

"Yes, Dr. Baker, this is Beau."

"Thanks Jimmy. Poor Beau got a nasty cut across his neck while on a trail ride yesterday," Katherine interjected, pulling herself out of her melancholy moment.

"He's a good looking gelding, but I see what you mean about that neck.

He could do with a couple of stitches and I'll give him some antibiotics just to be safe."

"Whatever you think. Beau is obviously big, but he is one of my favorite boarded horses. For a green broke giant, he's a sweetheart and would walk thru fire for you if you asked him."

Jimmy turned the horse in the aisle so Beau's head was now facing Katherine and the Vet. "Thanks Jimmy, I'll hold him for Dr. Baker. Would you do two things for me?"

"Sure."

"First, check the book to see when Sammy is coming for her lesson today. I think it's at 9:30. If so, would you start grooming Dillon while we finish up here, but before you do that, would you run that errand we talked about earlier?"

"Ok, I'll take care of it."

"Thanks Katherine," Bob said as Jimmy exited the aisle.

"For what?"

"I know you're busy and I appreciate whenever you hold the horses for me. Of all the barn owners I work with, I'm the least concerned about my own safety when I come to your barn," he readied his equipment to treat Beau's neck as they spoke.

"Is that because we have the best behaved horses in the area?" She smiled, turning Beau's head away from the vet.

"No, it's because I know you have my back and won't let go even if they did blow," he replied, cleaning the wound on Beau's neck.

"I hear you. You know I'm a fanatic about safety. Good to hear it's appreciated!"

"I'm rarely around anyone's horse unless there's something wrong with it. So, even the nicest horse can get spooky around me when I'm the guy poking and prodding them. I swear, horses can smell me coming in the barn door."

"Better they hate you than me because I can keep you safe. If they hated my guts, there isn't anyone crazy enough to have my back!"

Just then, Jimmy interjected, "Excuse me Katherine. I ran that errand and your lesson will be here in 15 minutes. I'll get Dillon ready."

"Thanks."

"When are we scheduled to come back?" Dr. Baker asked, preparing an antibiotic shot for Beau.

Katherine pulled the list out of her pocket and checked. "I think next Wednesday. We have a new horse coming in next Tuesday that needs the normal tests run. You probably have us on the schedule for Wednesday, just in case the trailer is delayed. Why do you ask?"

"Beau is going to need a few more visits and since we're coming back out anyway, we can check on him while we're here. No need to make a special call if you can keep an eye on that wound in the meantime."

"Sure."

"Let's plan on next Wednesday and that'll give you a chance to meet Brandon. I'm going to give him the shot now," he said casually, making eye contact with Katherine for a moment.

"Good boy," she said in a very calm tone, turning the horse's head a bit more toward her, both so the horse would not see what was coming and to ensure the safety of the vet.

"All done."

"If you're done, I'll throw him back in his stall and get the first school horse. While I'm gone, I made a loaf of my homemade banana bread. I asked Jimmy to bring it down from the house. It's on my desk in the office, help yourself. The coffee is hot as well."

"Wow! As much as I would love to dig into that banana bread, there's no need to pull the school horses out of their stalls, we can give shots in the stall if that's OK with you."

"Sure, follow me." Within just a few minutes both horses had been vaccinated and the pair headed back to her office. Bob sat on the comfortable leather couch to the left of Katherine's desk. The banana bread prominently displayed on a plate in the center of the desk, neatly wrapped in cling film. Katherine closed the office door behind them.

"I'm looking forward to a slice of that!"

"Actually, the whole loaf is for you but I wouldn't say no if you wanted to share a slice with me. Even though I don't have time to bake very often, I want every visit with you to be special before you take off in that damned RV and start your life of leisure!"

"I'm happy to share a *small* slice with you. Actually, if you take the offer in Canada, you could be leaving before I do," he whispered.

"Nothing is decided so we have to keep this quiet. Of course, it's OK to tell Mary because I know you two don't keep secrets. But no one else."

"The trick to a good relationship is to NEVER keep secrets from your partner. EVER. Mary and I have been married for more than 40 years and I've never kept a secret from her. Not one."

"No Secrets at all? You take your coffee black Bob, don't you?"

"Black is good. In answer to your question, I've never kept a single secret from my Mary. No matter how terrible it may have been because I knew the first time I kept something from her, it would be the first step down a very slippery slope and there would be no way to turn the clock back, once trust was lost."

"Wow, that's amazing. Here you go," she handed him his coffee. Kate realized that her entire life in North Carolina had been nothing but a series of secrets. One worse than the last, but she resolved that she had no choice. *I guess it's better that I don't have anyone in my life because Bob's right, keeping secrets would've ruined it anyway.* Katherine then took a knife out of the counter drawer before heading back to her desk and plopping down in her old wooden swivel office chair that reclined slightly as she leaned back. She'd found it at a swap meet and had to have it because it reminded her of the one her father had.

Carefully removing the cling film, she pretended to slice the entire loaf into two pieces. "Whoa, you know I love you like a daughter, but not enough to give you half of my banana bread. This stuff is like gold to me!" They both laughed and Katherine cut two normal slices of the loaf, placing each on a plate and handing one to Bob who devoured it in short order.

"I'm going to miss all of this when I retire. God that is good," he smiled staring at the plate. "I think that is one of the things I'll miss the most about my practice."

"What? Getting to hang out in the offices of tall, really good looking women like me?"

"Tall? In most parts of the world Katherine McMahon, you would be considered a little person," he laughed.

"I beg your pardon. What I lack in vertical height, I like to think I make up for in charm!"

There was a knock on the door. "Come in."

"Sammy is scheduled in about five minutes and I have Dillon groomed. I'll saddle-up now."

"Thanks Jimmy, but don't saddle him. I'm going to teach Sammy how to tack up before we ride today," she said as Jimmy headed out of her office, leaving her alone with Doctor Baker.

"So Bob, tell me about the new vet. Does he really know his stuff?"

"I think you're going to like him. He's a good guy who took a few years off to help his parents on their family farm before going to Vet school. He's been out of school for a year or two working for other vets in his area up north and now he's ready to take on his own practice. In fact, he's about your age I think, mid-thirties?"

"That's close enough! Do you trust him?"

"So far, I like what I see."

"Well, if he has your seal of approval that's good enough for me! I hope you'll drop me a line or an e-mail or a text from time to time. Actually, don't text me, I never turn that damned cell phone on anyway," she laughed.

"Ok, I won't text but you can count on lots of e-mails and postcards. Mary and I are not leaving for another month, besides, once you meet Brandon, I'm pretty sure you'll forget all about me."

"Not a chance," she carefully wrapped the banana bread as they both stood, before giving him a big hug.

"I'll see you on Wednesday."

"Bye Bob. Thanks for coming out. Say hey to Mary," Katherine called out to him as he disappeared into the parking lot, cradling the loaf of banana bread under his arm.

CHAPTER 3: JIMMY, THE PARADOX

Katherine entered the aisle at 8:30 am, leading Brandy who she'd just finished working. The mare was still very green over fences. A strikingly good looking bay appendix mare with a white star, Brandy was a coming five-year-old who was already pushing 16hh and had plenty of jump in her for the show ring. Katherine had already ridden Jackson earlier that morning.

"I think the Johnsons will be pleased with how Jackson's going and he's sure to kick some butt this season over fences."

"That'll make them very happy, especially Lizzy if she gets to show him." Jimmy remarked casually as he slipped a halter on the mare and hooked her to the crossties to untack her.

Katherine grabbed her sweat jacket from one of the hooks that was in front of each stall. "I'm expecting Lizzy to show him. With those long legs of hers, she'll look great on him, unless her dad steps in and says no. He can be a bit of a worry-wart when it comes to Lizzy's safety and that grey is a big, strong gelding that could get her in a lot of trouble if she's not paying attention. Well, you already know that." Katherine smiled, removing her thin, black leather riding gloves and neatly tucking them into the waistband of her body hugging breeches as she'd done hundreds of times over the past six years.

"For a big boned horse, he's got a lot of speed. Remember the day I opened him up in the field, just to see what he had under the hood?" Jimmy reminisced with a smile on his face that went from ear to ear as he removed the saddle from the mare's back and walked it into the nearby tack room.

"Oh yea, that was a hoot. For a minute there, you looked like a rider at the Kentucky Derby," she laughed, heading down the aisle toward her office and the arena gate.

Jimmy was Katherine's right arm at Fox Ridge and she knew how lucky she was to have him there. He cut a lean frame with dusty brown hair and a heart as big as Texas, the state he hailed from. She knew he dreamed of riding on the track, but was too big to ever be a jockey and too small to escape the bullying of classmates throughout his school years. It seemed that he got the *short end* of the stick in more ways than one.

As he came out of the tack room, Jimmy laughed, "Galloping full out on a horse like Jackson is like putting a motorhome on a race track and opening it up! Running Thoroughbreds on the track is more like racing a Maserati. Jackson may not have been built for speed but he is powerful and a lot of fun at a full gallop."

"I think you'd enjoy any horse as long as it was going full out! You know, Brandy's coming along nicely too. She's miles behind Jackson in her training, but she might be ready to haul to a few shows this season." Katherine leaned against the wall, enjoying her first cup of coffee for the morning that she brought down from her house in a thermal mug earlier.

"You mean you'd show her over fences this season?"

"No. She's still too green for that, but she'd be ready to put in the warm-up arenas and hack on the grounds, to get her some mileage at different venues. If she shows promise, we could take her to some open shows, just for the experience." Katherine casually watched Jimmy as he untacked the mare. She couldn't help but worry about what would become of him if she took the job in Canada. As with all the important decisions in her life, she'd held her cards close to the vest, carrying the weight of the world alone. *I can't give Jimmy or anyone else something to worry about, unless I decide to take the job,* she reasoned...*and besides, I'm worrying enough for everyone. I've got a few weeks to make up my mind and a lot can happen in that time*. Katherine couldn't possibly know how prophetic that thought was.

"I checked the book for the day and after Major, you have two more horses to ride before lunch and then you've got four lessons this afternoon," he said standing in the aisle brushing Brandy.

"It's surprisingly chilly this morning. Jimmy, do you want a cup of coffee to warm up?"

"No thanks, I picked up a cherry Slurpee when I got the paper this morning on my way in. With it being so cold this morning, at least I don't have to worry about the flies getting into it."

"Holy crap, it's cold enough to see your breath. How can you drink that stuff with ice in it this early in the morning?"

"I might ask you the same question. I love starting the day out with the newspaper and a good, stiff, cherry Slurpee at 5 a.m." Jimmy put the mare back in her stall and pulled Major out to start grooming him.

"You're a Texas boy through and through. Blue jeans, cowboy boots, hard drinking Slurpees first-thing in the morning and you keep up on current events by reading the paper. You're a paradox for sure Jimmy."

"What the heck is a paradox?" he asked while cleaning Major's hooves.

She caressed the warm mug in both hands, "A paradox is from the Greek word 'paradoxon' which means contrary to expectations, existing belief or perceived opinion. You, Jimmy are a Paradox and I couldn't be happier because of it." She set down her coffee mug on the rail and put on her thin black leather riding gloves, followed by her helmet. Katherine carefully tucked in her long auburn pony tail before securing the harness. "Jimmy, don't forget, I'm catering lunch at noon today for you and the staff."

"Wow! Now that's a paradox!" Jimmy exclaimed while bridling the horse.

"No paradox. You know I like to do a lunch for the staff at least once a month," she replied, aware that if she took the job in Canada, this would be the last lunch she would share with her staff.

"I'll be there!" he said, tightening the girth before bridling.

"After lunch, I'm heading over to the women's shelter for a meeting and then to the sheriff's office to drop off a flier, but I'll be back in time for my afternoon lessons."

"You sure do spend a lot of time at the women's shelter." Jimmy observed as he continued his work.

"Everyone should volunteer somewhere, it's good for the soul and it's a great way to remind you of just how lucky you are," she smiled thoughtfully while leaning against the rail enjoying her coffee.

"You might be right about that. By the way, speaking of the sheriff, I think he has a crush on you." Jimmy quipped.

Katherine laughed, "I think you've had one too many cherry Slurpees. Mac Cameron has more important things to focus on. Besides, every *single* woman in the county is after him and a few of the married ones as well. Between running Fox Ridge and the volunteer work I do, I don't have time for a man in my life. Hey, did you know Mac's running for re-election this year?"

"Yup, I read it in the paper last week."

"You really do read the newspaper?"

"Religiously, don't you?" Jimmy asked with a touch of sarcasm in his voice as their eyes met.

"Sorry, I must admit, I don't read the paper or watch the news. All too depressing for me. I thought you got the paper just for the crossword or the funnies."

"No, I read the paper to expand my knowledge of the world and then I do the crossword and read the funnies."

"While I'm gone this afternoon, would you check the schedule to make sure the horses I have booked for this afternoon's lessons are in from the field and ready to go?" she asked while heading down the barn aisle toward her office.

"Don't worry; I'll have everything ready. You can count on me."

"I know I can always count on you and that's one more thing I'm grateful for. By the way, I had Sarah text everyone else and asked them to be here at noon for lunch. You know, I have no clue how to use that damn cell phone."

"I'm pretty sure you're the only adult on the planet who still doesn't know how to use their cell phone." he laughed.

"Every time I try to text on that thing, it never works. What baffles me is why it's called a *smart phone. Now that's the ultimate oxymoron* because there's nothing smart about that phone." Jimmy just shook his head.

"You know, I could teach you how to use it if you wanted."

"No need. As long as I have you or Sarah around, I never need to learn how to use that damn thing!" Katherine set her coffee down on the rail and removed her sweat jacket before following Jimmy as he led the gelding into the arena. After they arrived in the center of the ring, Jimmy checked the girth one final time before giving Katherine a leg-up.

"Thanks," settling into her saddle while gathering up her reins, Katherine pulled the fob out of the pocket of her breeches and clicked it to once again turn on the stereo. Her choice of music for this horse, Lenny Kravitz.

CHAPTER 4 : GRATITUDE LUNCHEON

The barn staff was buzzing with anticipation over the catered luncheon being thrown for them. Noon couldn't come soon enough and when the staff finally headed outside, they found a beautifully dressed table under the front awning of the barn waiting for them. The table provided a wonderful view of the fields across the lane and the amazing fall colors on the hillsides. The large centerpiece of fresh cut autumnal flowers made the table elegant and inviting in the mid-day sun. As the group took their seats, Katherine stood up to make a toast.

"First, please give a warm welcome to Sheila Banks our caterer for this important luncheon today." Katherine started to applaud and the staff followed her lead.

"Thanks, it was my pleasure. I hope you enjoy your meal," Sheila smiled with pride while wiping her hands on the towel neatly tucked into the string belt of her blue and white striped apron with her embroidered business logo prominently displayed. Sheila opened **Banks Catering** the year after Katherine arrived in North Carolina. They two met at the local Chamber of Commerce monthly get together the month after Sheila opened her business. About ten years older than Katherine, Sheila shared her life with her husband and a grown daughter away at college. Struggling with empty nest syndrome when her only daughter left for college,

Sheila decided to redirect that angst into a new business venture and it was proving to be a great success.

"Ok then, for this month's luncheon, I'd like to celebrate how grateful and thankful I am to have each of you in my life." Katherine raised her water glass.

"Here, Here." Carl shouted as he raised his glass. Carl Taylor, a strikingly good looking, talented riding instructor in his 30s was exceedingly popular with his female clients and... all of his clients were female. He was known as the *barn flirt* and women flocked to him like bees to honey. Always impeccably dressed in black, tight fitting stretch breeches, knee high hunt boots that were polished to perfection, sporting an array of colorful pastel polo shirts that showcased his *guns* and deep tan. Of course, his clients didn't know that the tan came out of a bottle but that was just the first of his many little secrets. Either way, he was irresistible to the ladies. He smelled of wonderful cologne and had quickly become one of the most *in demand* riding instructors for *women of a certain age* in the area.

"Before we eat, please indulge me and let's go around the table to share the things you're grateful for. I know Thanksgiving is more than a month away, but I'm feeling especially grateful these days, so I'll start us off. I'm grateful for each of you, for this farm, for my life, for the friends I have in this town and for all of our success. I couldn't have done any of this without all of you." Katherine said thoughtfully, tears pooling in her eyes as she raised her glass, very aware that if she took the job in Canada, she would be long gone before Thanksgiving. The staff cooed with sentiment. "Jennifer, why don't you go next?"

Jennifer Collins, a slim, tall young woman in her late 20s with beautiful long blond hair, legs that wouldn't quit and on top of everything, she was very well-endowed. Jennifer taught Western riding and was part of the show team at Fox Ridge. She loved cowboys, country western music and fast cars. She rose with glass in hand, "OK. Let's see. I'm grateful for my boyfriend Troy, of course, for my parents, for my little brother, for my aunts and uncles and especially for my job. You know my monthly truck payment and insurance are huge."

"Here, Here," Carl said, holding up his glass again. "My turn," he insisted flamboyantly. His tall muscular frame made him look like something off the cover of a romance novel. "First I'm grateful for Sheila who created this beautiful luncheon soiree for us. It's almost as beautiful as she is." Sheila stood quietly a few feet from the table, quite touched by his recognition. Her dark shoulder-length hair was neatly tied back, creating a strong contrast against her ivory colored skin and crystal blue eyes, making it impossible for her to hide the fact that she was blushing.

"Leave her alone Carl," Katherine joked, rolling her eyes. The pair exchanged knowing glances.

"Well, I am grateful to her and she is beautiful. OK then. I'm grateful for all the women who ride with me, who insist on buying me gifts and allow me to spend time with them during their riding lessons and afterwards back at my trailer. And I'm especially grateful for the fact that their husbands have no interest in coming to watch their wives ride." Carl stated graciously as the table erupted in laughter. It was a well-known fact among the staff that Carl was the resident *housewife whisperer*. There wasn't a middle-aged, lonely housewife born that he couldn't seduce. Although he was a talented instructor, Carl had been flirting for so long that he believed his students were only riding with him for that reason.

"Thank you Carl for that inspiring toast." Katherine quipped as the group was still laughing. Still smiling from ear-to-ear, Carl took his seat. "Jimmy, your turn."

Jimmy picked up his glass and stood. "I'm grateful for Katherine..." he said simply, as he made eye contact with his boss who was clearly taken by surprise. "When no one else would give me a chance, Katherine did and I'm grateful. Working here means everything to me."

"Jimmy...thank you for that," she replied quickly, nearly losing it as Jimmy sat down. Katherine regrouped and called upon Sarah for the final toast. Sarah Browning was the Girl-Friday of the barn. She answered the phone, handled the books and pitched in wherever and whenever she was needed.

"Sarah, what are you grateful for?" Jennifer asked. Sarah stood with glass in hand. Her beautiful, long brunette hair tied back in a neat pony tail showcased her round face. Sarah used to love to ride as a girl but was now slightly overweight and more importantly, she carried the *weight of the world* on her shoulders. She was a jeans and cowboy boots kind of girl who preferred T-shirts and baseball caps over breeches and hunt boots. As a young woman of only 31 years, she had two young children, a husband and a lot of responsibilities. She found it all but impossible to get back to her pre-baby weight and while she knew that riding would help her shed the pounds, for the first time in her life she also knew fear. The kind of fear that comes when you have people counting on you. The kind of fear that makes women put their own dreams on the back burner because they're afraid of letting people down or being thought of as selfish. Now that Sarah had children, she found herself operating from a place of fear and while she hated it, she couldn't argue that it made perfect sense. If something happened to her, where would her family be?

"I'm grateful for a loving husband, for my two kids who I love more than life itself and…oh yea, for the chance to work with Jimmy!" She smiled, blowing him a kiss humorously from across the table.

"Ahhh, shucks Sarah, I never knew you cared." The table erupted in good humor.

"Well, now that we've all shared what and who we're grateful for, let's dig in." Katherine announced. The team enjoyed a plentiful meal of bar-b-que chicken, cornbread, coleslaw, green beans and a fabulous chocolate sheet cake.

CHAPTER 5: MARRIAGE?

After their delicious lunch, Sheila handled the clean-up while the staff returned to work and Katherine headed into town to meet with Barb Tomas, the Executive Director of the women's shelter. As a young girl, Barb stayed in a shelter back in Detroit with her mother and three siblings after her father went to jail. It took them a long time to get back on their feet and she was forever grateful to the shelter that helped them during that *rough patch,* as she referred to it. Barb saw running the local women's shelter as a way of paying it forward and she was proud to do it.

"Katherine, thanks for coming by. I'm dying to speak with you about the fundraiser." Barb stood smiling as Katherine entered her office, still dressed in her riding gear.

"Hi Barb," Katherine placed a large foil-wrapped package, the size of a football on Barb's desk before the pair hugged warmly and sat down.

"What's this?"

"I brought you a piece of cake." Katherine knew that Barb was a big fan of desserts and made sure she saved her a conspicuously large piece from their catered lunch.

"What a nice surprise! Did you bake this yourself? I hear your banana bread is legendary." Barb slid the package across the desk so she could check it out.

"Thanks, but no I didn't bake this one. I had lunch catered for the staff and thought you might like to have a little dessert."

"Brilliant! I've never met a dessert I didn't love. Wish I could say the same about men!" Barb chuckled, while intently unwrapping the aluminum foil to reveal the beautiful, large wedge of chocolate cake within. Her eyes lit up with delight. She was a thick woman of a certain age. Her grey hair made her look older than she actually was. Barb considered every gray hair a badge of honor that marked every lesson she had ever learned about life and she had no intentions of hiding her diploma.

"Who catered for you?" Barb eyes were transfixed on the cake like a wolf studying its prey.

"Sheila Banks from *Banks Catering* in Gaston. She's really good and not that expensive. Are you looking for a caterer?"

"I'm always looking for people I can rope into helping the shelter, you know that!"

"I'll e-mail her contact info when I get back to the barn."

"Great. So, let's talk about the fundraiser coming up next month. Can I count on you to sell raffle tickets at the barn and to bring the staff to help out?" Barb dipped her finger into the delicious frosting for a sampling.

"Absolutely. Jimmy, Carl, Jennifer and I will all be there. Sarah's going to stay back and take care of the barn."

"Are you sure you want to bring Carl after what happened the last time?"

"He can't help that he's a flirt and that the girls go gaga over him." The two women erupted with laughter.

"If they only knew which team he was really on, they wouldn't be so eager to flirt with him."

"On the contrary, I think if they knew, they'd like him that much more!" Katherine replied coyly.

"You know, you're probably right. I just don't like to see women fighting over a Trojan horse."

"While my Carl may be the poster child for Trojan in more ways than one, I think I can promise you that there won't be any girl-on-girl fights over him. Carl loves to flirt but he isn't crazy. God forbid two women did get into a physical fight over him, the winner would expect satisfaction and I'm afraid our Carl is all bark and no bite. As long as no one takes him up on his flirtations, he'll happily keep pushing the envelope. That's why he loves teaching married women. He can flirt all day long because he's counting on the fact that they wouldn't break their marriage vows."

"He hopes! If he wasn't so good looking, it wouldn't break my heart so much. You know, there's slim pickings around here." Barb giggled as she licked the icing from her finger.

"Are you looking for love?" Katherine joked, noticing how much Barb was enjoying the cake. "Look, don't stand on ceremony around me. Grab a fork and dig in. We're both women of the world and I know you can eat and work at the same time." Katherine quipped in a matter-of-fact tone.

"Thanks, I don't mind if I do." With that, she pulled a plastic fork out of her desk drawer and started to dig into the large piece of cake. "In answer to your question about whether or not I'm looking for a man...No. Hell No. I need a man in my life, like a need a hole in my head," she said as her fork dove with intent into the gorgeous cake. "After I divorced Louis ten years ago, I vowed to avoid marriage like the plague. Now, don't get me wrong, I wouldn't mind a few flings here and there but nothing permanent. In my experience, men are great for three things: sex, killing spiders and changing lightbulbs but not for much else. For God's sake, I run a shelter for battered women. I see what men are capable of every day, the last thing I want is to be married."

Katherine stared off across the room. "Kate? Earth to Kate."

"I'm here. I was just thinking...about the fundraiser," she replied absentmindedly.

"Speaking of good looking men whose bones I wouldn't mind jumping, I hear you and the Sheriff are an item." Barb's comment dripping with sarcasm. "Oh God this cake is good."

"I'm glad you like it. And, by the way, no, the Sheriff and I are just friends. At least, as far as I'm concerned. Mac Cameron has been a good friend to me since I came to town but I don't have time for a man in my life. Besides, I'm doing him a favor by *NOT* dating him. Coincidentally, I'm heading over to his office after our meeting today."

"Oooh, how romantic. You're stealing away for a little afternoon delight at the sheriff's office?" Barb leaned back in her office chair, holding the cake plate in her hand as she continued to enjoy her treat with abandon. "This cake is every bit as good as sex," she exclaimed. "What do you mean you're doing him a favor by not dating him?"

"There's no afternoon delight going on between Mac and me. Actually, Mac wanted some help designing a flier for his re-election campaign and to answer your question about why I'm doing him a favor by not dating him…my life's too busy, I'm married to my business so any man crazy enough to get into a relationship with me is guaranteed to be hurt."

"Kate, you're wrong. You would make someone a great wife." Barb said in a surprisingly serious tone, putting her fork down as she spoke.

"Thanks for that, but I know me better than you do. People like me should stick to working horses and the show ring where we know what we're doing. By the way, you have chocolate on the side of your cheek." Katherine said, her voice almost sounding sad.

"I hope I didn't hurt your feelings? I know you don't want a man in your life but I appreciate you stopping by to bring me the cake and for all your help with the event!" Barb wiped the chocolate frosting from her cheek and promptly licked it off her finger.

"You didn't hurt my feelings. It's not that I don't want a man in my life, I'm just not fit to have one in my life and…and…you're welcome." There was an awkward silence between the two friends for a moment before Katherine said, "Look, I have to run but I'll call you next week and maybe we can get together for lunch on Monday when the barn's closed." Katherine said as she got up from her seat, preparing to leave.

"I'm sorry Kate, really." Aware that she had inadvertently hit a nerve and possibly hurt her friend's feelings.

"It's OK, I better go. I'll call you about lunch."

"I look forward to it. Give Mac a big kiss for me." Barb said as she started to get up.

"You are the worst. Don't get up. Enjoy your cake and I'll call you about lunch."

CHAPTER 6: SHERIFF MAC CAMERON

K atherine parked her white dually in front of the Sheriff's office and grabbed the manila folder from the passenger's seat before heading into the historic two-story brick edifice, located in the middle of the downtown square. The building served as home to the sheriff's department and the courthouse. It was a beautiful old structure with wonderful dark woodwork throughout that Katherine adored.

"Hi Katherine, Mac'll be happy to see you!" Ruth smiled as Katherine entered the office. Ruth James had worked at the Sheriff's office for 10 years. First for Mac Cameron's predecessor for seven years and for the last three years for Mac. She was the glue that kept the place running smoothly for all those years and everyone knew it. Ruth was warm hearted, but loyal-to-a-fault when it came to keeping tight lipped about what happened in that office. She came from a family of police and firemen. Now in her 50s, Ruth was happy to have a desk job in the Sheriff's office while her husband drove truck.

"Hi Ruth, thanks."

Ruth pressed the button on her desk phone and dialed a few numbers before leaning in and saying. "Mac, Katherine's here....OK, I'll tell her." Ruth turned to Katherine, "He'll be out in a minute. Have a seat. Can I get you some coffee while you're waiting?" Ruth's fondness for Katherine was evident.

"No thanks, I just had lunch. How've you been?"

"The kids are fine and Jerry's doing day trips for the trucking firm now so we get to spend more time together. You know, he used to drive long hauls and we never saw each other."

"That must be nice to have him around more."

"You'd think, wouldn't you? Actually, I liked it more when he was on the road five days a week." Ruth whispered and the pair giggled. "Kate, you know that old saying, you can't live with em' and you can't kill em'?"

"Oh my God …I thought you were going to say, absence makes the heart grow fonder." Katherine gasped for a moment, trying to hide the dumfounded look on her face.

"You only thought that because you're not married for 25 years and you don't have kids."

"I know you're kidding, but you should never take your husband for granted Ruth, you're lucky to have a good one. I just came back from talking to Barb at the women's shelter. If you want to really appreciate Jerry, volunteer over there for a day or two and you'll find yourself over-joyed to be married to him and to have your family intact." Katherine said sincerely.

Ruth blushed, a bit embarrassed, "I know you're right. I think I'll go home tonight and give that boy a big ole' kiss."

"There you go and while you're at it, give him one from me too." The two women burst out in laughter.

"So Katherine, when are you getting hitched?" Ruth winked.

"No one in the world would want to marry me. Trust me, I'm no catch."

"You're so wrong. I know som ne who is very fond of you," Ruth declared coyly, rocking her head overtly toward Mac's closed office door. Katherine instantly blushed.

"Ruth!" she protested, as Mac opened his office door.

He looked quizzically at both women, "Did I miss something?"

"No…not a thing!" Ruth replied mischievously.

"…Kate, come on in, it's good to see you."

"Thanks." Katherine replied as she entered the office while Mac held the door for her, their bodies brushing as she passed him. Mac Cameron stood 6' tall, a well-built, middle-aged man who had been on the force for 20 years. First as an officer and now as Sheriff after winning the election three years earlier. He looked smart in his sheriff's kaki colored shirt, coal black hair, dark colored trousers with his fully outfitted belt that included cuffs and a loaded gun, among other things. He was the kind of man who had his uniforms tailored so he looked conspicuously handsome and powerful.

"Ruth, could you get me a cup of coffee and would you hold my calls for about 15 minutes? Kate, do you want a cup?"

"No thanks, Ruth already asked."

"I'll bring it in."

"Thanks," he said, closing the door behind him.

"It's good to see you," Mac said, hugging her tightly. "I've been so busy with the campaign that I haven't had time to come by. I miss spending time with you at the farm," he confessed, hugging her one more time before she sat down.

"Me too, but I understand you're busy. Hey, I drew up that flier you asked for," she pulled the flier out of its folder and placed it on his desk. "I also e-mailed it to you before I left the barn this morning so be sure to look for it in your inbox. What else can I do to help you with the campaign?"

"You can marry me!"

"...What?" She blurted out loudly.

"If you marry me, everyone in town will vote for me because they all love you and you would make me the happiest man on the planet." Mac stated plainly, sitting on the corner of his desk encroaching on her space, his eyes never leaving hers.

"Trust me, you don't want to be married to me, election or not," she exclaimed, trying to laugh it off but still shocked by his request.

"I would seriously get down on one knee and ask you to marry me right now if I thought you would say yes."

"We've talked about this before. I'm not marriage material, besides, I like our relationship as it is. Good friends are hard to come by and I appreciate what we have. I don't want to screw that up."

He took Katherine's hand, guiding her to her feet. "I want more than your friendship. I want you to be my wife." With that, Mac took her in his arms and kissed her tenderly. Katherine was stunned and thrown for a loop at his declaration. This was the first time they had kissed in the six years they'd known each other. Just then, there was a knock at the door.

Mac released her and took a step back, "Come." Katherine practically fell back into her chair staring at him, still in shock. She was grateful for the distraction to compose her thoughts. Mac had been her dear friend since she arrived in North Carolina and she didn't want to hurt him.

"Here's your coffee Mac," Ruth was suddenly aware of the awkward tension in the room.

"Thank you." Mac replied dismissively as Ruth exited the office and closed the door behind her.

"Look, I'm very fond of you but believe me, you don't want to be any more than friends with me. I work crazy hours, my time is never my own, my work is very dangerous and I could never give you what you deserve." Katherine whispered, hoping Ruth couldn't overhear the conversation.

"You just described my life, but I really think we could have something special. Why don't I come over on Sunday for dinner and we can talk about it."

Noticeably uncomfortable, "Mac, I don't think that's a good idea. Maybe we should just back off for a while," she said, rising from her chair to leave.

"What do you mean back off?" Mac grabbed Katherine by the wrist and pulled her to him, her arm uncomfortably wrenched behind her back as he held her close.

Surprised by the sudden change in his demeanor, Katherine whispered, "Mac, Ruth is right outside that door. Let's not ruin a perfectly good friendship." She was frightened by his behavior but didn't want to show it. She knew from years of working rank horses that as long as you kept your cool and continued to act like everything was fine, the horse need never know how frightened you really were. Her work had taught her the value of a good bluff. She often thought that horse trainers would make great poker players.

"I'm not trying to ruin anything. I just think we could have something very special. I've wanted you since the first time I met you six years ago. I've been very patient with you but it's time we took our relationship to the next level. Hell Kate, everyone in town thinks we're dating anyway," he said as he leaned into her, kissing her neck tenderly.

"Stop it. I'm leaving now," she demanded calmly, pushing him away from her with her free hand. "I'm going to leave the flier on your desk." Katherine backed away from him, looking him straight in the eye. "I want to be your friend. I don't have room in my life for a man. If being friends doesn't work for you, I understand but I don't have anything else to offer you," she said, grabbing her purse and keys and heading for the door.

"What about coming over for dinner on Sunday Kate, just as friends?" Mac asked, realizing his impetuous behavior crossed a line, scrambling to do some damage control now.

"I don't think that's a good idea. I don't want to put you in a situation on the farm that could get out of hand and ruin our friendship forever." She took a step back toward him, taking his hand in hers, looking him dead in the eye so there was no confusion, "You mean a lot to me. It's not you. It's me and my life that are the problem. Trust me, I'm saving us both a lot of heartache by stopping this before anything gets started. You mean too much to me as a dear friend to see you get hurt and if you get romantically involved with me, I promise you, you'll get hurt." Katherine headed for the office door, "Mac I hope you understand." As Katherine exited Mac's office she called out, "Bye Ruth," doing her best to sound cheerful as she quickly headed for the exit.

"You're leaving so soon?"

"Sorry, I have a full afternoon so I've got to get back to work."

It was very clear to Ruth that whatever happened in that office, Mac was unhappy about it when he barked at her, "Where are those damn monthly reports I asked you for this morning?"

"They're on the right side of your desk, in your inbox where I put them three hours ago."

CHAPTER 7: SHARON PINTER

Katherine called her best friend Sharon in New York for their normal Wednesday night video chat. Sharon was the only person Katherine stayed in touch with from her previous life in New York and the two had been friends since childhood. They met in school because their last names put them side-by-side alphabetically. However, when Sharon married Roger, she changed her name from McMasters to Pinter.

"Hey girl, you look great."

"Thanks, it's all that time I spend outside teaching and working horses. Makes for a great farmer's tan as long as I don't wear anything sleeveless! Did you change your hair color since last week?"

"Yea, I wasn't planning on doing it but Roger got that promotion we'd been hoping for so I decided to treat myself." Sharon tossed her hair back over her shoulder like an old-time movie starlet.

"Good for you! It looks great. How's baby Pamela?"

"Everyone's fine. Pam is growing like a week and Roger's over the moon this week since getting his promotion. He's been after that one for years."

"Tell him I said congrats! Is that a good thing for you or will he be working more hours?"

"He tells me it shouldn't mean more hours but it's more money, a better job title and another rung on that corporate ladder for him, so, all-in-all, it's great so far."

"I'm glad."

"So, what's been going on in your life this week?"

"I had to have another talk with Carl the other day."

"I love your Carl stories. Why are you rolling your eyes? This one must be a doozie. You know I love that guy. I've never even met Carl and I love him. What was it this time?"

Katherine laughed, "You know he's the biggest flirt in the world. Well, it's starting to get out of hand. Just about every lesson he books is with a lonely, middle-aged married woman looking for love and he's playing them all like fiddles." Sharon burst out laughing, rocking back in her chair in front of her laptop camera.

"Don't those women know he's gay?"

"Apparently not, and he's surely not about to tell them. So, meanwhile, he flirts with them to the point that they want to take their clothes off and jump his bones and then he leaves them high and dry. He tries to fix their hair and they think he's making a move on them but what he's actually doing is *fixing their hair because he loves doing hair*. You should hear him in his private lessons. He makes posting and using your seat sound like he's narrating a porn flick!" Sharon was howling with laughter by this point.

"I love this guy even more now!"

"Sharon, it's not that funny. I'm trying to run a serious riding academy and the last thing I need are angry husbands storming in to confront Carl because they think he's sleeping with their wives."

"I know, but you've got to see the humor in this. You're worried that some angry husband is going to confront Carl about sleeping with his wife and the reality is that there's a much better chance that Carl would hit on the husband. I especially love that Carl's a gay man hiding in plain sight. He's such a flirt that no one would ever consider that he might be gay. You have to admit, the guy's a genius," Sharon stated while trying to suppress her laughter. "When do I get to meet him? I feel like I already know him and I love him too!"

"You'll get to meet Carl the minute hell freezes over. As long as they know he's batting for the other team, I don't care how much he flirts with them, but by keeping it a secret, it feels like he's playing them and that bothers me. I'm never going to *out* him but he needs to come out of the closet before this gets out of hand," Katherine said seriously as Sharon continued to howl with laughter. "Stop laughing about it Sharon. You know I can see you!"

"Oh yea, I forgot! I get it. Ok… So what else is going on?" she struggled to compose herself.

"Let's see, Doctor Baker is going to officially retire next month."

"That's a shame, I know how much you like both he and his wife. Is someone taking over the practice?"

"Yea, he said he sold the practice to a younger vet named Brandon Stafford. Bob seems to like him and says he knows his stuff, so that's good enough for me."

"How much younger is the new vet?"

"I don't know. Bob guessed the new vet was in his mid-thirties. They're coming to the barn next Wednesday to work on a couple of horses, so I'll know all the poop then."

"Ohhhh, this could be someone for you to date!" Sharon clapped her hands with delight into the camera in her PJ's.

"He could also be married with 12 kids for all I know."

"Or, he could be single and looking for love…"

"Or he could be cross-eyed and look like a dog and weigh 500 pounds!"

"Until I hear to the contrary, I'm going to assume he's perfect and gorgeous and could be your knight in shining armor who will sweep you off your feet."

"Dream on! You know I've sworn off men anyway."

"If he's dreamy, maybe you'll change your mind."

"Let's talk about something else. Oh, I had a run-in with Mac Cameron."

"What happened?"

"He asked me to marry him?"

"Holy crap! You had to know that was coming. What did you say?"

"Thankfully, he was half kidding, but I know if I'd encouraged him at all, he would've asked for real."

"Would that be so bad? He's good looking, powerful, influential and he's crazy about you."

"Are you kidding me? You know that would be bad."

"You could be wrong. What happened with Dave wasn't your fault and it doesn't mean you can't have love in your life again."

"There's no way I would risk it. I would rather live alone forever, than risk that kind of heartbreak twice in a lifetime."

"You're going to have to find a way to close that chapter of your life and open a new one, and the sooner you do that, the better. Life's too short to live in the past. It's been six years and you aren't getting any younger."

"I did open a new chapter by moving here and starting Fox Ridge."

"Bullshit. I'm calling bullshit on that. You started a new business, but you're still emotionally stuck in the past. To the outside world, it might look like progress but you can't bullshit me or yourself. I've known you since we were kids. I want you to be happy Kate. Don't make the universe hit you over the head with a 2 X 4 to get your attention."

"Happy is a tall order for someone like me. I'm really glad you found Roger and you have the baby now but I don't believe that will ever be in the cards for me. I think my past has made that pretty clear. Speaking of Pamela, do I hear that adorable baby crying?"

"Yea I better run; Roger's out at his Wednesday night poker game so I'm mommy and daddy tonight...I love you Kate. Please open your heart to love, OK? If you'll just agree to be open to the idea, I promise you, the universe'll take care of the rest. Will you agree to do that?"

"I'll try. I Love you too."

"Oh, and give Carl a kiss for me!" Sharon giggled.

"You're a married woman for God's sake!"

"I know, so that makes me perfect for our Carl!"

CHAPTER 8: NEW BEGINNINGS

"Brandon, we have a pretty full day today. We're heading over to the Jackson Ranch to inoculate 25 cows and then over to the Smyth farm to check on a foal. After that we'll grab some lunch before heading over to Fox Ridge to run standard tests on a new horse that was supposed to arrive yesterday. While we're there, remind me to check on Beau's neck. After that, we're back here for office hours."

Brandon Stafford was only two years out of vet school, 6 feet tall with blonde hair, built like a quarter back, long and lean with some serious guns and just the right cut between his wide chest, trim waist and tight ass. Raised on his family's dairy farm, he was very experienced with large animals.

"Sounds like a fun day. If you want, I'll do the work and you can watch. We only have a few more weeks together before you're officially retired and I'm on my own anyway. I might as well start taking on the full load so I'm ready when you and Mary get into that RV and start living like hippies from the 60s!"

"I like the sound of that! Here, you might as well start driving your truck then," Bob threw the truck keys over to Brandon.

"Done." The two headed to their respective doors and buckled up before Brandon started off. "Do you want me to program the GPS before we leave the property?"

"Good idea. You can program the morning calls, but you won't need to program Fox Ridge because this truck knows the way to Katherine's place by heart."

"Who's Katherine? Somebody you have on the side that Mary doesn't know about?" Brandon smiled.

"Katherine's the best horsewoman I've ever had the privilege to know. She's a great trainer, teacher and a really good person. Best of all, she makes killer banana bread and like Pavlov's dogs, I salivate at the sound of her name."

"Wow, I can't wait to meet the lady. For you to be that crazy about someone, she must be special."

"She is. You'll see that I'm right when you meet her. I think you'll like her. Kate's been in the area for about six years. She came here from New York after her husband passed away. She's good people. Fair, but tough and expects everyone to be professional. I think she'll become one of your favorite clients too. She's always been one of mine."

Brandon envisioned Katherine to be a widow, possibly in her 70s, a well-seasoned, knowledgeable, cranky, opinionated horsewoman with lots of mileage and loads of grandchildren for whom she spent countless hours baking goodies. From the sounds of things, Katherine was probably Bob's peer.

The morning went along uneventfully. Brandon inoculated all the cows on the list before heading over to the Smyth farm to check on the foal. Afterwards, the duo stopped by the local drive-up window in town to grab some lunch.

"Mary, do you want us to pick up anything for you from the burger place?" Bob asked as he spoke with Mary from the truck on his cell phone.

"Thanks honey. Would you get me the usual?"

"Will do. We should be back in the office in about 20 minutes."

"I thought you were heading over the Katherine's?"

"We are, but we're both covered in cow shit and we stink to high heaven. We can't go to Katherine's smelling like a cow barn."

Overhearing their conversation, Brandon thought to himself, *Katherine must really be a high maintenance client if the vet has to shower in the middle of the day before going there. In every practice you have easy clients and you have hard clients.* He was eager to find out which category Katherine would fit into. Although, based on what he was hearing, it sure sounded like she was in the high maintenance category.

They ordered their food, headed back to the office, ate quickly, then showered and changed before jumping back in the truck to make the 20 minute drive over the Fox Ridge.

"Fox Ridge Equestrian Center, can I help you?" The voice on the other end of the phone asked.

"Hi Jimmy, this is Dr. Baker calling. Would you let Katherine know we're just leaving the office and heading your way? We should be there in about 20 minutes."

"She's working a horse right now but I'll let her know."

"Thanks, see you soon."

"Should I always call *Katherine the Great* before I head to her farm?"

"*Katherine the Great* is very fitting! I call ahead for purely selfish reasons and hopefully, you'll see why when we get there."

"Ok," Brandon replied a bit confused by Dr. Baker's cryptic answer.

Jimmy headed into the arena and turned down the music while he waited for a break in the training session. Katherine was working Brandy, her green jumping horse over fences while Jennifer looked on. "Katherine, excuse me," Jimmy called out. Katherine sat deep and executed a clean halt.

"Yea, Jimmy?"

"Dr. Baker called. He's leaving his office right now and heading this way. He said he'll be here in about 20 minutes."

"Thanks," wiping her forehead with her gloved hand. "Could you do me a favor?"

"Sure."

"Would you drive up to the house and pull the two loaves of banana bread out of my refrigerator and put them on my desk in my office?"

"OK."

"Be sure Sandy is out of my office so she doesn't get into them. You know she can't be trusted around goodies." Sandy was a stray beagle cross who showed up at Fox Ridge one day a few years ago. While she was a good companion and watch dog, she had her vices. One of which was sneaking goodies off of any unguarded plate she could find. "Jimmy, be sure to close the office door behind you so Sandy can't get in there. And you better not eat them either," she warned with a smile.

"I'll try not to," and with that, Jimmy turned the music back up and quietly exited the arena, allowing Katherine to get back to work.

"Can I ask you why you always make Dr. Baker banana bread? He's old enough to be your dad."

"I do it because he's the sweetest man I know and he helped me out in a big way when I first came here six years ago. I'll never forget his kindness and besides, he loves my banana bread. However, if he loved my cakes or my breads, I would make those for him as well. I don't ever want him to forget how much I appreciate him," she gathered up her reins and put the horse back out on the rail to resume work on her extensions.

"She's really coming along Katherine. Do you think she'll be ready for the next show?"

Katherine answered as she pushed the horse into a big extended trot, "I think she'll be ready for a couple of easy classes but she'll really need a lot of mileage on the show grounds so we can get her seasoned. Let's take our time on this first show and give her a chance to build her confidence."

"Sounds good. I'll check the show bill to see what classes will suit her and we can go from there."

"Great. Look for flat classes in the afternoon. I don't want her rushed out of the trailer and then thrown into an early morning class," Katherine's eyes were focused ahead as she drove the mare forward from her seat.

"Nice extension."

"I'm happy with her progress so far," Katherine said as she brought the mare back down to a walk, giving her a loose rein and patting her firmly on her neck. "Good girl." The mare pulled for all the rein she could get and stretched her neck happily at a flat-footed walk.

"I'm going to work on some fences before we finish up on her today. Can you keep an eye out for Dr. Baker and let me know when he arrives? Oh, and crank up the music on your way out, will you?"

"Will do," Jennifer said as she left the arena and headed to the front of the barn only to see Mrs. Klassen standing at the office door waiting for her. "Hi, Mrs. Klassen, I'm glad you could stop by."

"What is it Jennifer?" She asked abruptly, careful not to touch anything dirty in the barn.

"Come on into the office where it's quieter." The pair entered the office and Jennifer closed the door behind them. "Tommy's new to Fox Ridge and we need to talk about how he conducts himself in the barn."

"What do you mean? I raised my son to be a southern gentleman," she said, obviously very uncomfortable in the building and now with the assertion.

"He's often wired up when he comes here to ride. He likes to run around and he's really loud. My concern is that he's going to spook a horse and get himself or someone else hurt. So, I want to ask you two things as his mom; first, I need you to lay off the sugar before he comes to ride, and the second thing is that we have a list of barn rules that I would like you to review with him at home to give him a head start before he comes for his lessons."

"Jennifer, are you suggesting that my Tommy is a problem? You know, he's a gifted child."

"I'm sure he is, but Katherine is a stickler around here for safety and she mentioned that Tommy was running around in the barn the other day and we can't have that. So, if you could do these two things for me, Tommy will have a long, enjoyable, safe time riding at Fox Ridge. Thanks for coming by, I have to run. Here's a copy of the barn rules. Have a great day," and with that, Jennifer picked up the show bill for Katherine and headed out to the arena, leaving Mrs. Klassen speechless. A minute or two later, she read the barn rules and promptly stuffed the piece of paper into her purse and stormed out of the building, slamming the door behind her loudly.

CHAPTER 9: SPARKS

D
r. Baker and Dr. Brandon Stafford arrived at Fox Ridge Equestrian Center just before 1 pm. They parked near the front door of the massive dark brown metal building with its silver colored metal roof. As the pair grabbed their gear and headed into the barn through the *people door,* Brandon was overwhelmed by the sounds of Lenny Kravitz playing *Always on the Run* loudly in the riding arena, the guitar riffs bouncing off the metal walls.

"Hi Dr. Baker," Jennifer called out to the two men.

"Hi Jennifer, good to see you. I'd like you to meet Dr. Brandon Stafford. He's going to be taking over my practice in a few weeks when I retire, so he'll be coming on calls with me until then."

"I'm sorry to hear you're leaving. Dr. Stafford, welcome to Fox Ridge." Jennifer shook Brandon's hand, distracted by how good looking he was.

"Thanks Jennifer. Please call me Brandon. Do you always crank up the music in the barn during the day?"

"Oh that, Katherine's a big fan of Lenny Kravitz, Santana and Eric Clapton. Today, it's Lenny. She refers to it as her *secret weapon* for desensitizing green stock for the show ring. She also believes it helps them settle into a rhythm over fences. So, will you be coming to the awards banquet this weekend?"

"Yes. Dr. Baker was kind enough to invite me to go. I'm looking forward to it." Jennifer studied Brandon like a hawk studies a bunny rabbit. As a horsewoman, she routinely studied the build of the horses she came across. It was a quick way to determine their suitability for a particular job. After a quick study of Brandon Stafford, she was certain he would be suitable for some serious time in the sack. It took her a minute to get her mind back in the game.

"…Great. It's the party of the year. I better let Katherine know you're here."

"There's no need to interrupt her," Dr. Baker interjected, able to see Katherine jumping fences at the far end of the indoor arena.

"She specifically told me to let her know when you arrived and if I don't, she will have my head."

Wow, Katherine the Great must really be a pill, Brandon thought to himself. *She has everyone around here jumping and she's into Lenny Kravitz. What a strange choice of music for an elderly widow* he thought.

"Jimmy, do you know which horses Dr. Baker is working on today?"

"Yea. I'll get the first one now."

"Thanks," Jennifer headed across the arena toward the petite rider on the massive horse that had just jumped a big fence, making it look effortless.

"Katherine, excuse me. Dr. Baker is here with Dr. Stafford," Katherine sat down on the mare and brought her to a halt.

"Thanks. Jennifer, will you cool out the mare and put her up for me? Good girl. She's really coming along over fences." Katherine said while catching her breath and patting the mare on the neck.

"Sure." Jennifer waited in the middle of the arena as Katherine rode over to her before dismounting. Brandon watched her every move, fascinated by how tiny but nimble the elderly woman was. Jennifer moved close to Katherine as she stood, adjusting the stirrups for Jennifer's much longer legs and whispered, "Oh my God Katherine, I think I'm in love."

"I'd hope so, you've been dating Troy for a year," they continued in whispers to avoid being overheard.

"No, I mean with Dr. Brandon Stafford. Oh my God, he's gorgeous."

"What about Troy?"

"Dr. Stafford could be my *hall pass*. You know, in relationships when each person gets to sleep with the man or woman of their dreams without destroying their normal relationship."

"Are you nuts?"

"Wait until you meet him, he's gorgeous and he's charming. I'd take a hall pass for him any day."

"Get on the horse already!" Katherine said as Jennifer giggled like a school girl. Katherine gave her a leg-up before turning toward the men at the other end of the arena.

So, that's *Katherine the Great*, Brandon thought to himself. *She's little, but much stronger than I would've expected.* Katherine pulled her helmet off, shaking her long auburn hair loose as she walked across the arena toward the gate leading into the aisle. The trancelike guitar music still playing loudly in the background. She tucked her helmet under one arm, pulled the fob out of her breech pocket and shut off the music as she neared the two men.

"Bob, it's always a pleasure to see you," she exclaimed while placing her helmet on the rail then hugging him warmly. She took a moment to tie her hair back into a pony tail with a scrunchie she'd pulled out of one of the pockets of her black breeches that were so well tailored they appeared to be painted on. Katherine looked smart in her well-polished hunt boots, breeches and pink polo shirt. Brandon noted that the inside leg of both boots were well-worn, likely from hundreds of hours in the saddle.

"Katherine this is Dr. Brandon Stafford...he's the vet I told you about who will be taking over my practice in a few weeks," Dr. Baker said proudly.

Katherine turned her attention to Brandon, removing her riding gloves and slipping them into the waist band of her breeches. Looking him dead in the eye, she shook his hand firmly. "Brandon, welcome to Fox Ridge. I hope you'll think of us as family," and with that, she drew him in gently and hugged him warmly just as she had Dr. Baker.

Surprised by her warmth, he barely managed to hug her back. "Th...anks. It's good to be here." Katherine was only 5'4", petite with a firm handshake, vibrant auburn hair that fell just past her shoulders and the body of a gymnast. She was nothing like he'd imagined and he was grateful to have been so wrong. Brandon was completely distracted by how beautiful she was and by how attracted he was to her the minute they met.

"Before you get started, you have to come into my office for a minute. Do either of you want a cup of coffee or a soda?"

"None for me, I just ate lunch," Dr. Baker said.

"No thanks," Brandon chimed in.

"There's something different about you Bob, you look especially sharp today. Have you two been to the spa or did you just take the morning off?"

"Actually, Brandon and I worked cows all morning. We showered after lunch so we wouldn't stink up your barn."

"You're the most thoughtful man I know," Katherine smiled at him over her shoulder as she opened her office door. There, on the desk were two loaves of banana bread, each wrapped in cling film.

"Wow, Katherine, did you make those for me?" Dr. Baker asked with delight in his voice.

"Actually, I made one for you and one for Brandon."

"How did you know...?" Brandon asked, surprised, studying Katherine, finding her even more attractive by the minute.

"Bob told me last week that you'd be joining him today. I want you to feel as welcome in the community as Bob and Mary made me feel when I first got here."

"I do...Thank you," Brandon said sincerely.

"It's nothing, just my way of saying welcome home," she smiled up at him feeling a warmth deep in her gut. A feeling she had never felt before around any other man. At first, it made her nervous but she had to admit, it felt good.

"Katherine's famous for her banana bread. I'm addicted to it, so I'm hoping you'll tell me you don't like bananas so I can take that loaf off your hands."

"Sorry but I love banana bread."

"Damn," Dr. Baker replied and the trio laughed.

"Bob, how's Mary? Is she getting excited about your retirement?"

"She sure is. Speaking of my Mary, I need to call her to see if we have any last minute calls for this afternoon."

"No worries, we'll take good care of Brandon while you're gone,"

Katherine smiled at Brandon when she noticed he was staring at her with a peculiar look on his face. "Brandon, are you OK? You look a bit peeked." She whispered to him.

"...I'm fine," struggling to get his mind back on the job and off the beautiful woman in front of him. His mind was racing with thoughts of how attracted he was to her. How he would like to spend time with her and much more.

"Good, then come with me. There's someone special I want you to meet." She took him by the arm and headed down the barn aisle. "Brandon, let me introduce you to Jimmy Weston, the best barn man in North Carolina," Katherine said with pride. "Jimmy, this is Dr. Brandon Stafford." The two men shook hands warmly. "If I'm not around, Jimmy can get you anything you need. He's the best."

"Thanks," Jimmy beamed with pride.

"It's good to meet you. I'm looking forward to working together."

"Thank you Dr. Stafford. It is good to meet you too."

"Please, call me Brandon."

"Ok," Jimmy was surprised that a veterinarian was willing to work on a first-name basis with the barn help.

"Brandon, you're so lucky to be working with Bob. No one made me feel more welcome than he did when I first came to town and I'll never forget his kindness."

"He's a great guy. You know, he's very fond of you too."

"He is?" She feigned surprise.

"In fact, I have to admit that the way he spoke of you and your skills and your personality, I assumed you were very tall and at least 70 years old and a legend of some kind."

Katherine and Jimmy both burst out laughing. "I'm overwhelmed, but far be it from me to contradict an adoring fan." Brandon found himself studying Katherine. For some reason, he couldn't take his eyes off of her. Overwhelmed with a feeling that he knew her or more appropriately that he wanted to know everything about her. He found himself wanting to touch her, to kiss her. He'd never felt that way when meeting any other woman and he was finding it hard to concentrate on the job at hand.

When Bob returned a few moments later, Katherine said, "Gentlemen,

I have a horse to work but I wanted to see my favorite vet and now, my two favorite vets! I hope you both enjoy your banana bread," Katherine hugged Bob first and then Brandon. This time, Brandon hugged her back. She felt warm and safe in his arms for some unknown reason. Before she left his embrace, their eyes met for a single moment. Something magical happened. She could feel sparks deep in her core. Something she'd never felt with any man before. It was a warm feeling that felt good, but it also made her nervous.

Dr. Baker broke the obvious tension, "Katherine, I'll say good-bye now and we'll let ourselves out when we finish pulling the blood on the new horse. I'll give you a call…I mean Brandon will give you a call with the test results in a day or two."

"Great. It was good to meet you Brandon."

"Same here and thanks again for the banana bread." Katherine couldn't remember any man ever looking at her in that way, as though he knew her intimately. As though, he knew her heart. She'd spent the last six years hiding her emotions and Dr. Stafford appeared to have seen through it all with just one look. Katherine was frightened but at the same time, there was no denying, something deep inside was stirring.

The two vets finished their work in about 15 minutes and headed out to their truck, carefully cradling their loaves of banana bread like they were cherished babies. Brandon stopped in his tracks noticing Katherine riding in the outdoor arena. He lifted the loaf to his nose to fully drink in the wonderful smell.

"She's not only beautiful but she's good people and she cleans up good too, but you'll see that at the banquet," Dr. Baker said as he got into the passenger's side of the truck. "We've got office hours to get to Brandon. You can't stand here all afternoon staring at Katherine."

CHAPTER 10: CARL THE CASANOVA

Madeline Smith sat atop Butterscotch, the large chestnut school horse at a halt on the rail as Carl stood in the center of the ring. As usual, he cut a dashing figure in his black hunt boots, form fitting black breeches and pastel polo shirt. All of which show-cased his beautiful well-muscled, tanned body and he knew it.

Madeline, in her early 50s, married to the head of a large corporation for more than 25 years, couldn't say she was happily married. Instead, one could say that she was looking for happiness. Her husband traveled a lot and she was an empty nester with both of her children in college. After her first lesson with Carl three weeks ago, scheduled on a lark after a girl-friend recommended it, Madeline started booking lessons several times a week. On the surface, it looked like Madeline was very serious about improving her riding, but not necessarily horses.

"Madeline, today we're going to talk about the posting trot. Posting to the trot was originally done to reduce wear and tear on the rider when the horse was in second gear – the trot. However, when done properly, the posting trot can be used for so much more. It'll shorten your horse's back, collect him, extend him, control his speed and so much more," Carl said with a glint in his eye, using his hands as he spoke.

"Great, I like the idea of being able to control his speed. Where do we begin?"

Carl slowly approached her on the rail, never taking his eyes from hers. She swallowed hard as he got closer. His slicked back, coal black hair made him look almost like a Spanish matador. "Madeline, it's very important to have your legs in the right position in order to take full advantage of the power between your legs during the posting trot." He stood close, looking up at her on the horse. He placed his right hand on her thigh and smiled when he heard her gasp. He then placed his left on the heel of her boot and gently pulled her heel down. He could see her face turn red, her lower lip quiver. "While gripping with your thighs Madeline...you know how to grip with your thighs don't you?" She nodded obediently, "I want you to sink into your heels, just like this. Can you feel that?" He asked with a sly smile as he pulled down on her boot heel gently, squeezing her thigh at the same time.

"Yes, I can feel everything...," she stammered, her voice cracking, her breathing quickening.

"When we post to the trot, I don't want you to just go up and down, I want you to rise up and thrust your pelvic plate forward and back, forward and back, forward and back. Let the beast between your legs do the up and down and you thrust forward and back and between you, you'll create a rhythm that works. Watch me and I'll show you."

With that, he turned sideways, bent his knees slightly and started to slowly thrust his hips forward and back. He placed one hand on the front of his pelvic plate and the other in the small of his back. "Do you see what I'm trying to do here Madeline?" He smiled up at her.

"...Yes...I believe I do," she answered nervously. Carl's large muscular biceps were ripped and his strong thighs filled out his breeches nicely. It was something that Madeline did not overlook during her riding lessons. Carl straightened up and came close to Madeline again.

Reaching up, Carl placed his hand on the small of her back and said, "Madeline, while you're at a standstill, I want you to grip the horse with both thighs, rise up slightly and thrust forward with your pelvic plate while I hold the small of your back so I can feel the thrust." She did as instructed, her face flushed as the horse took a step forward.

"Oh, I didn't know he was going to move," Madeline yelped, a bit surprised, pulling back on the reins quickly.

"Good Work! When you thrust properly, you control the beast between your legs more effectively and it gives you more power. Madeline, isn't more power and control something that every woman wants over the beast between her legs?" He winked at her.

"Why....yes.... I'd like to have more power and control," she said, knowing this conversation was no longer about posting to the trot.

"Then I'll teach you everything you need to know and you shall have it. I don't know if I've mentioned this to you before, but riding is a metaphor for life."

"I can see that. I like the sound of having complete control over everything between my thighs," she said, her face now very red, her voice shaky.

"Excellent! Let's take him out on the rail at a walk and practice posting. When he's actually trotting, he'll push you up and down as he goes, and that'll make it easier for you to post, however, until you get the hang of things, I want you posting only at the walk." She squeezed gently and Butterscotch stepped off obediently. "As in all things in life, when both parties are doing their part, finding a good rhythm is easy, however, when one partner isn't doing their share, it makes it harder for the other partner to find a good, enjoyable rhythm. Do you know what I mean Madeline?"

"I know exactly what you mean," she said confidently. Carl recognized that Madeline was referring to her marriage.

"Ok, forward and thrust, forward and thrust, forward and thrust," Carl said, imitating the movement himself on the ground.

"Wow, this is harder than it looks," she said a bit breathlessly.

"Once you settle into a rhythm, you'll be surprised how easy and natural it is and once you feel that rhythm, you'll have complete control. The posting trot is like so many things in life, when you stop resisting, it all falls into place. The greatest gift I can give to you today is to get you so thoroughly exhausted you can no longer resist and when you get to that place, you'll settle into a natural rhythm and your natural urge to thrust will take over," Carl said with a mischievous smile. "Do you understand what I'm trying to say Madeline?"

"...Yes... I think I do," she said breathlessly as she continued to post at the walk. Madeline's husband traveled so much that she found herself alone most nights. Hearing Carl speak to her this way, she was sweating heavily. While the physicality of posting at the walk was exhausting, it wasn't the only reason why she was so over heated.

After a few more strides, Carl said, "Madeline, sit deep and halt your horse please," she responded immediately, thankful for the break.

As Carl approached her, she could feel her face heating up again. Excited, but trying hard not to show it, Madeline was certain he'd touch her again at any moment. He came very near to her and whispered, "One of the things to watch as you learn how to post is that your hands must be able to move independently so you're not interfering with the horse's mouth as you thrust with your hips." He took her hands in his as she held the reins and said, "Try posting as I hold your hands still, so you can feel the difference."

From a standstill, posting was nearly impossible to do but Madeline gave it her best effort. Her hands were low on the saddle. As she thrust her hips forward. They touched his hands. She felt awkward and excited at the same time. Carl had taught enough lessons to enough women to know exactly what he was doing. "Can you feel that Madeline?"

"Yes...I can," she said, gasping for breath.

"Does that feel good?"

"...Yes, it feels very good," she whispered.

"Excellent, Ok, now sit," and with that, he released her hands and once again positioned his hands on her thigh and the heel of her boot. "Remember to keep your legs long and heels down at all times so you're well anchored and safe. I don't want you to fall off."

"Neither do I!"

"Before you get too sore, let's call it a day." With that, Carl turned and headed to the center of the arena with Madeline following him. She dismounted in the center of the arena while Carl held Butterscotch's reins, standing on the left side to make sure Madeline dismounted safely.

"You did great today," Carl slid his hand down her back as she stepped off the horse. He could see her jump at his touch and he smiled.

"I'll see you on Friday." She whispered with a smile.

"Perfect, we'll work some more on perfecting that thrusting motion."

CHAPTER 11: SAFETY IS NO ACCIDENT

"**M**orning Jimmy," Katherine called out as she entered the barn early that morning.

"Good Morning," he replied, moving a wheelbarrow down the aisle.

"Before I forget, we have a new volunteer coming by tonight. Would you mind helping her get settled in?"

"No problem, what's her name?"

"Brenda Ashford. She's Gracie's aunt."

Katherine headed into her office to check her schedule for the day and to do the weekly payroll. "Would you ask Jennifer to come in to see me when she gets here?" Katherine called out from her office.

"OK."

A few minutes after making coffee and writing the payroll checks for the week, Jennifer knocked on the door frame.

"Hi Katherine, Jimmy said you wanted to see me?" Jennifer inquired with a bit of concern in her voice.

"Morning Jenn, come in and close the door. Do you want some coffee?"

"No thanks."

"Have a seat." Jennifer nervously settled into one of the chairs across from Katherine's desk.

"Jenn, I've asked you before to focus on teaching safety in all your lessons but when I walked into the barn yesterday afternoon, there were three of your young students running around in the indoor. One of them was Tommy Klassen. I know he's a new student for you but we can't have that inside the barn. They're going to spook a horse and get someone hurt."

"I'm sorry but they were just playing," Jennifer's apology sounded luke-warm at best.

"There are two sports in the world in which playing around at the wrong time can get someone killed in less than 30 seconds; skydiving and horseback riding. In my teaching career, no one has ever gotten hurt on my watch and I intend to keep it that way. I'm a stickler for safety and I expect the same from you. Having your students running around the barn like maniacs puts everyone's safety in jeopardy and I need you to know that if someone gets hurt on your watch, I'll fire your ass in a New York minute. Do I make myself clear?"

"Perfectly."

"You and I both know that horses are no more dangerous than a dog but they're over 1000 pounds that can easily kill someone if they're spooked or jacked around with. You know the safety rules of this barn and it's up to you to teach those rules to all of your students. By the way, you should know that any injury claims will run up my insurance rates forever and if that happens, I'll take it out of your hide!" she smiled.

"I got it and I'm sorry about the kids, I'll sit them all down and spend some time focusing on safety."

"Don't spend *some time* focusing on safety, all of your time needs to be focused on safety. I don't want you to scare them, but I expect you to teach them how to act properly in the barn. By not setting high safety standards and respecting the safety of others, you're putting your student's in harm's way. If you don't start focusing on safety in every lesson, I'll do it for you. Are we clear on that?"

"Perfectly clear."

"Thanks for coming in. By the way, how's Troy?"

"Thanks for asking! We fight more than we probably should but I sure do love him. He's the closest I've come to finding 'Mr. Right'."

"Are you looking for Mr. Right?"

"I think so. It would be nice to be married and have kids."

"I agree, it would be nice…" Katherine said, her thoughts drifting off for a moment to a very dark place. "Well, I've got some work to finish here in the office. Say hi to Troy for me when you see him."

"We have a date tonight so I'll be sure to tell him. He's taking me to a special restaurant to celebrate our one year anniversary as an exclusive couple."

"Good for you! I hope you both have a great time."

"Thanks and I'm sorry about the kids."

"Don't be sorry. Just fix it." Katherine said, looking up from her paperwork.

CHAPTER 12: OUR NEW VOLUNTEER

L ater that evening, "Jimmy, this is Brenda Ashford, Gracie's aunt. Brenda was nice enough to volunteer to help us prepare for this weekend's show."

"Nice to meet you." Jimmy smiled shaking her hand as he had with hundreds of other visitors to Fox Ridge Equestrian Center over the years.

"Good to meet you Jimmy. So, what can I do to help?" Brenda asked keenly, her short blonde hair fit perfectly with her small, gymnast like, petite body. She was about two inches shorter than Jimmy and they made a nice looking couple Katherine thought to herself as they spoke.

"Jimmy, can you be Brenda's mentor this week?"

"Sure," he replied casually, not paying too much attention to the new volunteer.

"Brenda, you're in good hands with Jimmy. If you have time to come to the barn each evening this week, by Friday, you'll be a capable barn person. Jimmy'll take good care of you and thanks for volunteering. It means a lot to the kids and to me."

"I'm happy to come all five nights this week ahead of the show, if that's OK with you Jimmy?

"Sure, that'd be a big help Brenda."

"I hope you still feel that way by Friday." She laughed. "Ok, Jimmy, so what do you want me to do first?"

"Let's go into the tack room and we can clean some saddles while we talk about the other things we'll be doing throughout the week in preparation for the show."

"Lead on, I'll do anything you want." The pair headed into the large tack room where there were easily more than 20 saddles neatly displayed on wall mounted racks lining one side of the room. Under the bottom rack was a tack trunk and on the opposite wall were dozens of neatly hung bridles. The spacious room also had a table and four chairs as well as several free standing saddle racks and stools. A steep set of wooden stairs leading up to the hay loft above were situated in the furthest back corner of the expansive tack room.

"Brenda, if you'll grab a saddle rack and stool you can set them up close to the table, I'll get you a saddle to work on."

"Do you want me to get the saddle down?"

"I'm afraid you're too short to reach. I'll get it for you."

"Ok," Jimmy brought over a beautiful English saddle from one of the racks on the wall. He carefully removed the girth and stirrup leathers after setting the saddle on the free standing rack in front of Brenda. He placed the fittings on the table.

"Make yourself comfortable while I get a saddle to work on and we can do the saddle cleaning together."

"I'll get you a rack and stool," Jimmy was touched by how helpful Brenda was being. He returned in a moment with a second English saddle and again, placed it on the free standing rack in front of his stool before carefully removing the girth, stirrup leathers and irons and placing them all on the table.

"Brenda, the goal of this exercise is to first, inspect each piece of leather looking for any excess wear. Once we get past that, we'll clean everything and condition with oil."

"Why are we putting oil on the saddles?"

"They're made out of leather and leather is basically skin so, after giving it a good scrubbing, we need to recondition the leather so it doesn't get dry and crack… it's kind of like washing your skin thoroughly and then putting moisturizer on afterwards."

"Are you looking at my crow's feet?" she laughed. Jimmy leaned in close to carefully look into her eyes.

"I don't see any crow's feet…" he replied honestly. The two shared an awkward silence for a moment before Brenda spoke, realizing that Jimmy didn't connect that she was joking.

"So, how long have you worked at Fox Ridge?"

"A little more than five years now. Before that, I worked as a vet tech for Dr. Baker. In fact, that's where Katherine and I met."

"What do you mean?"

"Dr. Baker was treating a horse here and he needed Katherine to swing by the office to pick up some medicine for the animal. She came into the office and we started talking and the rest is history."

"Do you mean she stole you away from Dr. Baker?"

"No. It was Dr. Baker who suggested I call her for a job because he knew I loved working with horses and he's really fond of Katherine. He thought we would get along really well and he was right."

"Are you and Katherine an item?" she smiled, very interested in his answer, while moving the saddle rack closer to her chair.

Jimmy laughed loudly, "No, I think of Katherine like my older sister… don't let her hear you say *older* or she'll get cranky." Jimmy started to demonstrate how to clean the saddles as Brenda studied him from her stool on the other side of the table.

"Would you like some rubber gloves for your hands?"

"Not unless you think my hands will hurt the saddles."

"I don't usually use gloves but I thought as a girl, you might want to protect your fingernails."

"I don't have to worry about my manicure because I'm a physical therapist. So my hands have callouses and it's impossible to keep long nails in my line of work. See…" She extended her open hand to Jimmy across the table. He held her hand, running his free hand over the inside of her palm, only to discover she wasn't kidding about having callouses.

"Wow, your hands are almost as calloused as mine.":

"Let me see," and with that, Jimmy flipped his own hand over. Brenda held his hand in hers and rested her free hand against his palm, drawing a circle with her fingertips.

"You're right!"

"Where do you work?" Jimmy asked, as the pair started cleaning their saddles in earnest.

"At the hospital."

"Do you like what you do?"

"Yes, but it's not what I really want to do with the rest of my life."

"What's that?"

"What I really want to do is start a Therapeutic Riding Center so I can help people heal and connect them with horses at the same time."

"What got you interested in that kind of work?" Jimmy asked while keeping his attention on the saddle cleaning.

"I have a niece who's physically challenged and she loves horses."

"Do you mean Gracie? She seems fit as a fiddle."

"No, not Gracie. She has a sister who spends most of her time at home because of her physical challenges. If I had a Therapeutic Riding Program, Carol could be in the barn with the horses and focus on healing her body at the same time." Brenda's voice cracked a bit as she spoke of her niece.

"Brenda, what's wrong?" Jimmy was no longer focusing on the saddle in front of him but now his attention was on Brenda.

"I love Carol so much... that's my niece's name, Gracie's sister. She's kind and sweet and funny and sometimes, I just don't think it's fair that she's burdened with physical challenges." Brenda said, thoughtfully staring down at the saddle in front of her as she rubbed the leather with her sponge filled with saddle soap. "I worked with a Therapeutic Riding Center for five years before I moved here. I was a volunteer and did just about everything at one time or another."

"How many different jobs could there be at a Therapeutic Riding Center?"

"I was a side-walker, a leader, I went for my certification and I spent a lot of time in the office helping with the books and the paperwork. I also did community outreach, cleaned stalls and helped host events. Watching those students transform physically and mentally was as rewarding and healing for the volunteers as it was for the students. I wish there was a Center in this area so Carol could participate because it breaks my heart to think she'll spend the rest of her life unable to run or jump or play or ride horses like other kids."

"I know what you mean. Sometimes life doesn't seem fair at all."

"Jimmy, I appreciate the thought but someone like you couldn't possibly understand what it's like for someone like Carol. You ride horses for a living. There's probably nothing you can't do."

Their eyes met across the table. Jimmy had a perplexed look on his face, "I think I understand more than you might think."

"How so?"

"My dream has always been to run Thoroughbreds on the track, but I was born too tall. Can you believe I was too tall to do anything?" He smiled. "My backup plan was to train and show hunters, but for that job, I'm considered too short for the Hunter show ring. So, instead, I help Katherine prepare show horses for their tall, long legged owners, most of whom have no idea how lucky they are. So, yea, I think I have some idea of what you're talking about." Jimmy once again began to focus on cleaning the saddle.

"Jimmy, I'm sorry." Brenda said, reaching over to touch his hand. Jimmy stopped his work. He glanced at Brenda's hand on his before looking up. Their eyes connected again for a moment. He could see that she really did understand how he felt.

The pair shared a silent moment before Jimmy asked, "Would… you like a soda?"

"Sure. Thanks. Anything diet is Ok with me."

"I can't stand the taste of diet soda. How do you drink that stuff?" Jimmy asked as he got up and headed across the room to the refrigerator to get a diet soda for Brenda and a regular soda for himself.

"I hate the taste of it but I have to watch my weight. Just like you feel you got the short end of the stick because of your height, I come from a long line of chubby women, so, I do my best to keep that monster at bay and diet soda is one of the ways I try to do that. I guess, at the end of the day, everyone has something about themselves they're unhappy about. You know, though, it's all relative, isn't it?" she said casually as she watched Jimmy approaching her with two sodas. "The short legged person who feels they got ripped off by life is looked on by the person in a wheel chair as someone who is frivolous and the chubby person is probably looked on with envy by the really skinny person who can't figure out how to keep weight on."

"I never thought of it that way, but I think you're right. Here's your soda." Jimmy said while setting down the diet cola in front of Brenda's work area at the table.

"Thanks."

"So, you're saying I should be grateful that I have legs and can ride, instead of feeling like a got short changed by the universe because I'm not 6'2"?"

"Yup. You know, my grandmother once told me when I was a kid that there are no good days or bad days, just days...and there are no good breaks or bad breaks, just events in life...what YOU decide they are, is what they'll be and it has nothing to do with what happened during the day."

"She sounds like a really smart person."

"She was."

"I'm sorry, did she pass away?"

"Yea, just last year. She was 85 and still sharp and smart and funny."

"You must miss her?"

"I try to focus on how lucky I was to have her in my life at all. That way, I don't spend time thinking about what I lost. There's an old Dr. Seuss quote that says: 'Don't be sad that it's over, be glad that it happened.'"

"I don't get it?"

"It means, instead of choosing to focus on what you lost, focus instead on how lucky you were to have had that event, job or person in your life at all. In other words, when something ends, you can choose to focus on the loss or you can choose to celebrate everything that happened before the loss. I try to focus on how lucky I was to have my grandmother in my life for all those years, rather than focus on how I was cheated when she died at 85."

"I see what you mean. I think you're right." Jimmy found himself studying Brenda. She was smart, insightful, funny and for the first time, he actually noticed how good looking she was. He was used to working with a lot of volunteers and after a while, they all looked the same but Brenda was different. Brenda was someone Jimmy liked and he liked her very much.

CHAPTER 13: MY FAIRY GODMOTHER

Wednesday night, Katherine called Sharon in New York via online chat to catch up on each other's lives as they had done every Wednesday evening for years.

"Hey Girl"

"Hey Girl, I'm dying to find out about the new vet. Is he fabulous?"

"Good to see you too and yes, I'm fine. Thanks for asking!"

"Ok. Fine, it's good to see you. OK, so, tell me all about the new vet," Sharon insisted, rubbing her hands together with glee.

"You're a hoot. I can tell you're dying to know all the details but first, I have some other news."

"What could possibly be more important than the new vet?"

"I think Jimmy has a crush on one of our new volunteers!"

"I've never actually met Jimmy but I think of him like my little brother. From everything you've told me over the years, Jimmy's the sweetest Texas boy ever so I'm thrilled that he might have found himself a good woman. I assume she is a good woman, isn't she?"

"She's the aunt of one of my students. Her name is Brenda Ashford. She's a Physical Therapist who volunteered for several years at a Therapeutic Riding Center, loves kids, is not terribly familiar with horses but she's a hard worker and really nice. Plus, she's shorter than Jimmy, really pretty and they seemed to hit it off really well."

"That's great. Has he asked her out yet?"

"No, but I'll keep encouraging him to do so. I think they're adorable together."

"Sounds like love is in the air at Fox Ridge. So, tell me about you and the new vet."

"Ok, so he's very nice."

"And…?"

"And, he likes banana bread and he's good with the horses. What else do you want to know?"

"Don't act obtuse! Everybody likes your banana bread and he was trained to be good with the horses. You know what I really want to know…do you want to sleep with him?"

"You're a married woman. What the hell is up with you?" The pair laughed.

"I may be married and I may be a new mother, but I'm still a woman who's turned on by good looking men and I want to relive my romantic years through you. I've been on pins and needles all week, so, tell me all the poop!"

"I'll say this…he's not ugly. In fact, Jennifer practically had an orgasm just looking at the guy. She told me she wanted him as her *hall pass*."

"He must be good looking if Jennifer wants to use him as her *hall pass*. Oh Kate, romance and sexual tension are SO wasted on you for God's sake. Did you at least take a photo of the guy so you can send it to me?"

"Yea, I asked a complete stranger to give me an hour so I could figure out how to turn on my damn cell phone and then figure out how to take a picture of the guy. There's no chance he would've thought I was a crazy stalker…of course, I didn't take his picture."

"Did you at least find out if he's married or not?"

"Shit, I forgot to ask a total stranger what his marital status was. So, that explains why I'm still single! I should have asked him while he was treating one of the horses or maybe while we were doing his photoshoot. What was I thinking?" Katherine said, slapping her hand to her forehead in an obviously overt, sarcastic gesture.

"You're a smart woman. Was he wearing a wedding ring or did he have a tan line on his left ring finger?"

"I don't know. Wow, now I know how you got Roger. That poor guy didn't stand a chance with you on the prowl."

"I'm a woman who knows what she wants and isn't afraid to go after it. So what can you tell me about him? There has to be something!"

"There was something weird about him. Brandon looked at me like he knew me. It creeped me out at first. He was sort of staring at me a lot," Katherine said plainly.

"That's a good sign! It means he was captivated by your beauty!"

"You're delusional. I felt like he could see right through me. Like he knew about my past. Even my friend Mac, the local Sheriff who wants to marry me has never looked at me like that."

"Maybe that's good? I mean, at some point you're going to have to tell someone about your past in order for you to move forward with your life and since Brandon's going to be your vet, maybe he's the guy."

"There's not a chance in hell that I'm going to tell anyone in North Carolina about my past. That's why I'm thinking about taking that job in Canada."

Sharon took a deep breath and sighed, "You know how I feel about that job in Canada and you know I think you should stop running from your past but OK…let's talk about something else. Do you like the new vet?"

"Yea, I like him. Oh, and by the way, he's coming to the banquet over the weekend."

"Great! That'll give you a chance to get to know him outside of work. What are you wearing?"

"I hadn't really thought about it."

"What? You have to wear something fabulous. Ohhh, I have the perfect dress for catching a man. It's this great backless dress made of satin. It's black and slinky all the way to the floor," Sharon exclaimed with delight, her voice filled with excitement. "I'm going to get it so you can see it, I'll be right back." She quickly got up from her seat and ran out of the room for a moment.

A short time later, Sharon reappeared holding a beautiful, black satin, backless gown with white piping to accentuate the big scoop in the back of the dress and tiny spaghetti straps. "Holy crap Sharon, that's gorgeous!"

"I agree and you're going to wear it to the banquet! I'll Fed Ex it to you tomorrow. You have to wear it! It screams…baby, come and get some 'shuggga'!"

"You don't have to do that. Besides, what if you need it?" Katherine felt embarrassed and pathetic that her best friend was going to have to send her clothes.

"If you're ever going to find a man, I have to do this. No arguments. Besides, there's no way in hell I can wear this dress since I had the baby. On you, this dress is going to cause a riot. On me, it's going to look like ten pounds of bologna in a five pound sack. Besides, you're my best friend and it's my job to be your wing woman. When's the banquet?"

"This Saturday."

"Great. I'll pack up the dress and head into town in the morning to overnight it to you along with some goodies to go with it. Everything should be there in plenty of time. This is such fun! Do you have any high heeled shoes?"

"No! I have hunt boots, wellies, casual flats and tennis shoes."

"OK, I'll send along some shoes to go with it. What size are you?"

"Seven and a half."

"They'll fit. I'm an eight, but that's close enough! Gee Kate, I feel like a proud mamma getting her daughter ready for her first prom. No, I feel like your Fairy Godmother or better yet, I could be the Good Witch in the Wizard of Oz and you're Dorothy. Oh, what are you going to do with your hair?"

"I don't know. Tie it back I guess," Katherine replied in complete defeat but with a smile on her face. Although Sharon was like a bulldozer when she was excited about an idea, Katherine appreciated her support more than she could say.

"You can't just tie it back. This is what I want you to do with your hair." Sharon demonstrated a French bun using her own hair and turning her head so Kate could watch. "Do you think you could do that?"

"Yes. I can do that," Katherine replied smiling, aware that Sharon wasn't asking her, she was telling her.

"Be sure to stop and get a bunch of bobby pins, you'll need them and while you're at it, get some hair spray. Oh, and the most important thing you'll need for your big night out in this dress is a box of condoms."

"What?"

"When Brandon sees you in that dress, the need for contraception is going to come up, literally and figuratively. You're a grown-ass woman who needs to think of these things before the need *comes up*, if you get my drift."

"I don't even know if Brandon is available. He could be married with 10 kids for all I know. Anyway, isn't a guy supposed to have those things in his wallet at all times and since when do Fairy Godmothers push girls to get condoms?"

"Whether it's Brandon or some other fabulous man at the banquet, I'm a 21st century Fairy Godmother. We use cell phones, FedEx, Skype and we preach safe sex. Brandon has no idea what you're going to do to him in this dress so there's no way he could possibly be prepared. Just get some condoms. Ohhh...do you have someone there who can hem the dress?"

"I think Sarah can hem it for me. I know she loves to do that stuff. I'll ask her not to cut any of the material, so we can return it to you as it was when it arrived. We might be able to use that iron on fusing stuff so we don't have to use a needle on that fabric."

"Great idea! We're about the same size but you're so much shorter than I am. In fact, you're much shorter than everyone, so you're definitely going to need to work on the hem. Be sure to have her hem the dress while you're wearing the heels because I'm sending the tall ones. Call me the day of the event and I'll check you out before you leave."

"Do I have to wear stilts for shoes?" Katherine bemoaned.

"It's not my fault you're a shrimp. You'll wear the shoes and you'll turn every head in that ballroom when they see you in this dress. Get used to it, you're going to blow every man away on Saturday night. All that riding and work in the barn has produced a body to die for. This dress will show that off bigtime," she laughed with glee.

"OK, Fairy Godmother, for you, I'll put my hair in a bun, wear the hooker dress and I'll wear stilts! I'll call you on the web before I leave for the banquet. We're planning on leaving around 4:30, so I'll call you around 4:15. Will you be around?"

"I will now!"

"I better get going. Sharon, thanks for all your help. Can I at least pay for the shipping bill?"

"Absolutely not! This is my early Christmas present to you. Not the dress…my early Christmas present to you is the man you will reel-in while you're wearing that dress."

"You sure are confident about the power of that dress."

"Trust me, any man who sees you wearing this dress is going to lose his mind. This dress, when worn by someone with a body like yours, is like a W.M.A., weapon of mass attraction."

"I know I complain a lot, but I really do appreciate everything you do for me and I'm thinking of you as my Fairy Godmother now! You're the best."

"I know you do. I love you Kate! Your Fairy Godmother will be waiting for your call on Saturday and don't forget the condoms."

CHAPTER 14: LOVE IS IN THE AIR

"**K**atherine, can I talk to you?" Jimmy asked early the next morning while he and Katherine were grooming the first two training horses of the day.

"Sure. What's on your mind?"

"I was working with Brenda the other night cleaning tack and she told me that Gracie has a sister named Carol who is physically challenged. She was pretty upset about how unfair it was."

"I agree, it sucks. Did she say what the disability was?"

"No, but I was wondering...do you think we could invite Gracie to bring Carol to the barn one day this week and put her up on a pony?"

"That's a great idea but I don't know anything about her physical disabilities or how to work with those challenges. I'd be afraid I might hurt her. What we need is someone who's worked with a Therapeutic Riding Center or someone who works with the disabled so they can help us know what to do and what not to do with her."

"Brenda is a physical therapist and volunteered at a Therapeutic Riding Center for five years. She's certified and she'd know exactly how to keep things safe for Carol. Would that work?"

"I think you sound like you've got a little crush on Gracie's aunt Brenda."

"WHAT? No, I just think she's really nice and wants to do something nice for her niece."

"Jimmy, for you, anything. Let me go check the schedule and see what day will work."

"That would be great. THANKS." Jimmy continued grooming the first horse on the book while Katherine headed into her office.

A few minutes later, she returned. "What do you think about inviting them to come out a week from next Thursday evening after school? My schedule is pretty clear and the barn should be fairly quiet."

"That's perfect! Thank you for doing this."

"Do you want me to call Brenda to set it up?"

"No need. She's coming out tonight to help get ready for the show. I'll talk to her then."

"Ok then, let's do it." Katherine replied with a smile on her face. In the nearly six years they'd known each other, she'd never known Jimmy to go on a date, so, the fact that he was expressing any interest in someone made her very happy. Even if love wasn't an option for her, she wanted Jimmy to find love.

Ж

Later that evening, Brenda arrived at the barn to find Jimmy waiting for her with a big Texas smile on his face.

"Hi Brenda."

"Hi Jimmy, what are we working on tonight?"

"Tonight we're packing tack trunks and cleaning out the trailers, if you're game."

"Absolutely, lead on."

"Hey, before we get started, I wanted to talk to you about something."

"Sure, what's up? You're not going to fire me now are you?" She laughed.

"No! You're doing a great job. Really!" Jimmy wanted to make sure Brenda didn't worry about being fired as a volunteer.

"Whew, that's a relief," She smiled at him, realizing he'd actually taken her seriously and didn't realize she was joking.

70

"I wanted to invite you to bring Carol and her family out to the barn a week from next Thursday night, if you're all free. After we talked, I spoke with Katherine this morning about putting Carol up on a pony and she was all for it, as long as there was someone qualified making sure everything was safe. I told her you were certified and that you were a physical therapist. She said she was all for it. So, what do you think?"

"Jimmy, I can't believe you did that for me." Brenda threw her arms around his neck, hugging him tightly and kissing him on the cheek. "Thank you so much. This means so much to me and I know Carol is going to love the whole experience."

Jimmy blushed and was speechless for a moment, paralyzed in place, "OK...then...let's plan on a week from next Thursday night around 5:00 pm."

"Sorry for being so forward, I'm just so excited." Brenda said, slowly releasing him from her arms and taking an awkward step back.

"You don't ever need to apologize for hugs or kisses. I'm like Sandy the barn dog, I can never get enough of those. Ok, we've got a lot to do tonight so we better get started. Let's head into the tack room and start packing the trunks."

Katherine was at the other end of the aisle smiling to herself as she watched Brenda hug Jimmy. *Poor Jimmy, he's so nervous he can't even hug her back. I'm sure he'll get the hang of it in time, all guys do.* Jimmy blushed so brightly that Katherine could see it from the other end of the aisle.

Ж

Later that same evening, "Fox Ridge, can I help you?" Katherine answered the phone while sitting at her office desk. She'd just finished teaching her last lesson of the evening and was going to sit down to do some paperwork before working her last horse of the day.

"Katherine, hi, it's Brandon Stafford." She felt an odd excitement, mixed with concern when she heard his voice.

"Hi Brandon, it's nice to hear from you. How are you?" Still concerned about how he'd looked at her the day before. Almost as though he'd known everything about her.

"Fine. How are you?"

"Better now than I was before you called."

"By the way, thank you for the banana bread. It was wonderful."

"I'm glad you liked it. You said it *was* wonderful, is there any left since I saw you yesterday?" She was starting to relax.

"I'm embarrassed to admit there's not a single crumb left. It went fast."

"I'll take that as a high compliment for my banana bread, unless you fed it to one of the animals in the clinic?"

"No, I ate all of it!"

"Then, I'll just have to make more for you the next time you come to the barn," she said honestly, happy that he'd enjoyed it.

"I'd like that," he said truthfully.

"Were you calling with the test results on our new horse?" While Katherine liked speaking with Brandon, she was torn between wanting to get to know him better while at the same time, keeping her distance.

"You'll be happy to know that all the tests came back negative. You have nothing to worry about, he's healthy."

"That's great news. I appreciate you calling with the results. I guess I'll see you at the banquet this weekend?"

"Yes...actually, Katherine, I'd like to ask you something, if you don't mind?" Brandon proceeded cautiously.

"...OK...sure Brandon, ask me anything?" After their initial meeting in the barn the day before, Katherine was fearful that Brandon might ask her something she wasn't prepared to talk about, but she'd lived the last six years bluffing her way through situations just like this.

"Are you...free for dinner tonight?" He inquired somewhat timidly.

There was silence on the phone at Katherine's end, "...I... ummm...Brandon."

"I'm sorry, I didn't mean to be forward or to make you uncomfortable. Please accept my apology."

"Wait a minute...I'm the one who owes you an apology," she said slowly, taken aback but relieved that he wasn't asking about her past.

"For what?"

"I've been here for six years and I must admit, you're the first man to ask me out to dinner. You just caught me off guard, that's all."

"I can't believe no one else has asked you out to dinner in all that time. You're smart and funny and gorgeous...ahhh, sorry, I don't mean to sound like a stalker."

"Never apologize for giving a woman a compliment! The truth is often stranger than fiction. I'm afraid to say, you're the first and I must admit, I'm very rusty at this sort of thing, so, if you'll grant me a do over, I'll say this; I haven't eaten yet but I'm obligated to stay at the barn until closing which won't be until 9:00 pm. However, if you don't mind having dinner here, I'd love to go out, or I guess it would be 'go in' to dinner with you Dr. Stafford, provided your invitation is still good?"

"Great! Yes. Do you like Chinese?"

"I love Chinese or we can order a pizza when you get here. Whatever you prefer since you're the one asking me out, or is it in?" She laughed.

"I'll pick up Chinese and be over in an hour."

"Perfect. I have one more horse to work and a new client coming by but I'll be done by the time you get here. We don't do alcohol in the barn but we do have sodas, bottled water, coffee or tea, if that works for you?"

"That works. Is there anything special you'd like?"

"I love kung pao chicken or anything spicy with chicken in it. I also like fried rice and egg rolls and by the way, if you're thinking I'm one of those women who doesn't eat, you picked the wrong dinner partner. I won't be offended if you want to retract your dinner invitation now. You should know that I can eat with the best of them!" Brandon laughed out loud over the phone. "Actually, I hadn't thought about it until this moment, but that might be the reason why no man has ever asked me out to dinner after all!"

"Good to know. I'm still coming with dinner in spite of that revelation, but now I'll be sure to bring enough so I don't leave you hungry. You know what they say about Chinese food. I'll grab a quick shower, pick up dinner and see you in about an hour. Oh, and I'll bring the reports on the new horse so Mary doesn't have to mail them to you."

"Great, it's a date. Bye Brandon." She felt immediate relief as well as a flutter of excitement deep in her core. It was an unusual feeling, something that she hadn't felt before and while it made her nervous, she had to admit to herself that she liked it.

CHAPTER 15: CHINESE TAKE-OUT

Brandon entered the barn about an hour later, freshly showered, shaved and wearing a clean, pale blue polo shirt and jeans that fit him almost too good. Katherine noticed him immediately. She was visiting with some new clients, having already finished working the horse. "Hi Brandon."

"Hi Katherine."

"Let me introduce you to the Bremertons, Dale and Colleen. This is Dr. Brandon Stafford, our new vet." Everyone exchanged cordialities before Katherine said, "Brandon was nice enough to hand deliver a report on a new horse we have in the barn and we're going to have dinner together."

"We don't want to keep you from your dinner," Colleen Bremerton said.

"Brandon, you're welcome to make yourself at home in the office. We're going to finish up here and I'll join you in a few minutes."

"OK, will do. It was nice to meet you Dale, Colleen." Brandon headed into the office, leaving the door open. He could overhear the conversation Katherine was having with the Bremertons as he began unpacking the food containers.

"Colleen, if you're looking to purchase your first horse, the one piece of advice I would give is to focus first and last on the character of the animal. I don't care what he looks like, what his papers look like or what barn he comes from, at the end of the day, it's a horse's character that's going to determine whether or not your relationship is long and wonderful or short and miserable. I often tell people that every horse, no matter what, is at some time going to be stressed out or spooked, just like people. When that happens, and the horse is figuratively *backed into a corner*, what comes out of that corner is going to be the true character of the animal. If you purchased your horse based on his fine character, you'll have no worries because he'll have your back. If you purchased your horse based only on his looks, registration papers or some sales pitch, what comes out of that corner is likely to be one big pain in the backside."

"I never thought about looking at a horse's character. I was always looking at his registration papers or markings because I thought his bloodlines would determine his character."

"We all know families with wonderful parents who ended up with terrible children. Bloodlines don't always determine character! Choosing a horse based on his character follows the same rules you should follow when choosing a mate. No offense Dale! If you choose your mate based on how good looking he is or on what car he drives or what college he went to, rather than choosing him based on things like, is he kind and thoughtful to you, is he a stand-up guy, does he do the right thing in life, you know, character issues – if you pick a man on any criteria other than good character, you're heading for a train wreck."

"Luckily for Colleen, she chose me based on my stellar character and I happen to also have a great car, job and good looks!"

"That makes you a triple threat for sure!" Katherine said as the trio shared a good laugh.

"Thanks for the tips! I think I got lucky with Dale. Now that I know what I'm supposed to be looking for in a horse, that changes everything."

"Happy to help. You've already done really well picking a good man, so, finding the perfect horse should be a snap. If you'd like some help shopping, give me a call next week and we'll set something up."

"Thanks for everything. I'll call you next week." Colleen extended her hand to shake Katherine's.

"We're huggers here at Fox Ridge. Drive safely." Katherine gently pulled her in for a hug and did likewise with Dale.

"Thanks again!" Colleen said enthusiastically.

"Enjoy your dinner," Dale called out to Brandon as the pair headed for the barn door.

"Thanks Dale!" Brandon replied.

A few moments later Brandon stood up as Katherine entered the office. She gave Brandon a warm hug. "Thanks for asking me 'in' to dinner," she said genuinely, their eyes connecting. He hugged her back, thoroughly enjoying the closeness. Katherine felt warm and safe in his arms again for some reason. It was a feeling she hadn't ever had in the arms of a man. She wanted this feeling to last forever. Katherine lingered happily in his embrace for what felt like a lifetime.

"Thanks for accepting my invitation. I left the report on your desk in the brown envelope," He whispered, noticing that she was staring at him, almost studying him.

"…Great. I just need to do one thing and then I'm all set for our dinner date. This is a dinner date isn't it?" Katherine scrambled to refocus.

"Yes, I believe we are officially on a date."

"I'll be right back," she laughed nervously before heading down the barn aisle. "Jimmy?"

"We're in the tack room. I'll be right out."

"Don't bother, I'll come to you." Katherine peeked inside the tack room to find Jimmy and Brenda packing tack trunks.

"Hi Brenda." Katherine had forgotten that Brenda was helping out for the week.

"Hi Katherine and thank you for allowing my niece to come to the barn."

"It's our pleasure. I know Jimmy and I are both looking forward to it! Jimmy, Brandon and I are going to be in my office eating dinner. Give me a holler if you need anything."

"Ok, will do," Jimmy smiled. He was glad to see Katherine so happy.

"Thanks. Good to see you Brenda and thanks for helping us out this week."

Katherine headed back up the aisle, noticing three boarders working their horses in the indoor before she entered her office. She closed the door behind her so they could eat in peace and sat down at her desk, making more space for them.

"I picked up everything you mentioned and some things I thought you might like to try. I didn't want to risk you leaving our first dinner date hungry."

"That's very thoughtful of you. Can I pay for at least half of this feast?" Katherine asked while running a hair brush through her hair and tying it into a neat pony tail.

Brandon looked up from his work, "Absolutely not! A gentleman never lets a lady pay on a date."

"Well then, grab a chair and let's dig in. What would you like to drink?" Touched by his comment, she walked by him to get to the small refrigerator next to the couch.

"Soda's fine."

"Do you want ice?"

"No ice for me. Right out of the can is fine."

"Geez, I'm starving now that I can smell it!"

"Great, I love a woman with an appetite." He smiled, enjoying himself very much.

"Well, I hope you mean that because you're having dinner with one tonight!" She said unapologetically, pulling sodas from the refrigerator while Brandon pulled the last container from the paper bag. Katherine leaned down close to him placing his soda on the desk. He liked the feeling of her body close to his.

"Your hair smells nice." Brandon said casually while arranging the boxes on the desk top.

"Thanks. I'm surprised you can smell my hair through all the horse shit I have on me by the end of the day!"

"I noticed that as well, but even with that, you smell great." Brandon managed to get his mind back on dinner.

"I have paper plates and plastic silverware. So, have you run into any tough cases since taking over the practice?" Katherine asked casually, while placing various foods on her plate. She was interested in learning more about the new vet who seemed to be able to see right through her.

Taking only a moment to consider the question, "Oh, yea, there's one that stands out that still gives me nightmares! Bob was out on an emergency call so I was on my own for this one. We have a cattleman in the area who wanted to extract semen from a new bull so he could artificially inseminate his herd. He thought he could save a few dollars by hiring me to come and draw the samples rather than hiring specialists who do nothing but semen collection."

"Holy crap, that's one of those situations that I warn my riders about."

"What do you mean?" He asked between bites.

"I tell them, if you're wondering about whether or not to do something risky around a horse, ask yourself this question...*do you think there's a good chance you'll have to explain it to an emergency room clerk*...if so, don't do it... So, how did it go?"

"Needless to say, it wasn't pretty, but thankfully, I didn't have to explain things to an emergency room clerk. Although, it was a sticky situation," Brandon stated, making them both laugh. Katherine was surprised and a bit wary of how easy it was to talk to this man.

"Is that a semen joke...you know, sticky situation?"

"Very funny!"

"So, how in the world did you get the job done without getting killed?" She asked between bites as she studied him.

"The trick is, and I found this out the hard way; apparently, you're supposed to excite the bull so he's ready to mount anything, and I do mean anything," Brandon explained using his hands in an overly animated fashion. "Ideally, you want to convince him that the phantom cow is a better date than you are so while he's mounting the phantom, you crawl underneath him to do the collection. You do know what a phantom is, don't you?"

"A guy who skips out on the dinner check when you're on a date?"

"No, I'm talking about the other phantom. The phantom I'm talking about looks like a vaulting apparatus you would see in gymnastics, except this one has a fake cow's head on it and some additional gear to help the bull do his business."

"Oh, you meant *that* phantom. So, how did the bull take to that phantom?" The two broke out in laughter.

"Honestly, I can't think of too many things in the world more dangerous than getting into a small, confined area with a big, hot-and-bothered one-ton bull that has horns and is sexually frustrated. I thought I was going to meet my maker that day!"

"Did you get the sample?" Truly interested to see just how tenacious Brandon Stafford was.

"Oh yea, I got the sample, but that's the last time I do that job. I prefer women and the thought of getting paid to excite a bull and then hold what looks like a giant condom on him to capture his magic juices, well, it's not a job I'm interested in doing twice in one lifetime." By this time, Katherine was howling with laughter as she visualized the whole event.

"Magic Juices? Did you at least buy him dinner before you took advantage of him?" she howled.

"No," he demanded. "I wasn't dating him, just milking him to get his semen." The two continued to laugh between bites.

"It's a pretty odd thing to do for a living isn't it? I mean, imagine being a kid and saying to your parents...when I grow up, I hope to be the guy who arouses one-ton bulls so I can stick their wiener into a giant condom and capture their magic juices," Katherine said in a matter-of-fact tone. Now Brandon was howling with laughter and choking on his food.

"Are you OK?" Katherine asked through her own laughter.

"Yea...I'm fine. I just never expected *Katherine the Great* to use the words wiener, giant condom and magic juices in the same sentence."

"*Katherine the Great*, where in the world did you get that from?"

"The way Bob spoke of you before we met, I imagined you to be like royalty, like *Katherine the Great*. Imagine my surprise when we actually met and you were young and short and nice and funny and warm."

"Thanks Brandon. What do you mean short? You know, now that you brought it up, I kind of like being called *Katherine the Great*," she said thoughtfully, tilting her head slightly as she looked at him smiling, holding her fork up like a scepter with a skewered pot sticker snared in the tines before eating it. Brandon was enjoying watching her eat. He realized that Katherine wasn't kidding when she warned him about her big appetite.

"So, Katherine, tell me about the music in the arena while you work a horse? What's that all about?"

"Please, call me Kate. I love Santana. Who doesn't? The rhythm of his music really works with the rhythm of a jumping horse. His music starts out steady and cool and then ramps up, which is perfect music to listen to while riding a course. Jumping fences is like dancing with a great partner, the better your combined rhythm, the better the ride. In fact, I use his music, Eric Clapton's and Lenny Kravitz's so often that when I'm in the show ring, it's running through my head, even though the music isn't playing. I never thought about it until this moment but all three of those artists are great guitarists. That's what I'm attracted to I guess. You'd think I would be attracted to great drummers because of the beat, but I'm a sucker for great guitarists. Keith Richards, from the Stones, is another one of my favorites," she said passionately.

"I didn't hear any music tonight when I came in. Were you working on the flat?"

"No, I worked the bay over fences but I had customers riding in the arena so I didn't have any music playing and the Bremertons were here as well. I only indulge myself when I'm the only rider in the arena. That's why Jimmy and I work most of the training horses before the barn opens in the morning. The funny thing is that my customers have no idea that I do this when they aren't here. I guess I'm like most people...one person in public and someone else in private." She could see that Brandon had stopped eating for a moment and was studying her. She smiled before taking another bite. "I know I could wear headsets but I want the horse to connect with the same music that I'm listening to and frankly blaring the music desensitizes my horses to any noise they may encounter in the real show ring, which gives me an edge. I'm the kind of girl who likes to be over prepared because when I get in the ring, I'm in there for only one reason...to win. My best friend says I'm very competitive. I don't think that's the case, I just like to win ALL THE TIME!" They both laughed.

"So, now that I've told you about my toughest case, what has been the toughest horse you've encountered since you arrived at Fox Ridge?"

"That's an easy one. We called him Wild Chuck. I think about that horse all the time because his owner nearly ended my career by getting me killed. Funny thing, I have no fear of big horses, but clueless owners scare the crap out of me!"

"What do you mean?"

"His owner assured me the horse was professionally trained. He was soooo wrong! Wild Chuck was the kind of horse that makes a trainer wake up in a cold sweat in the middle of the night. He was a 16hh, hot blooded crossbred, seven-year-old knucklehead who was, at best, green broke and had a bad attitude to boot because he was spoiled his entire life. So, he came into the barn to be 'legged up,' not 'trained.' It didn't take 30 seconds in the saddle to find out he'd never been ridden, despite the owner's promises to the contrary. He was especially dangerous because he was full sized, handy as a pocket on a shirt and certifiably crazy. Because of all that, I asked Jimmy to head him and weight down my off stirrup just to make sure the horse didn't go anywhere while I mounted. I used the mounting block to get on. I don't know if you noticed, but some people think I'm short?" She pointed out casually.

"I've heard that rumor a time or two," Brandon smiled while casually eating.

"Anyway, Jimmy was new to the barn back then and hadn't worked directly with a trainer before so we were still training him while I was supposed to be working the horse. At that point, I thought I was just legging up a broke horse so I figured it was a good chance to focus on training Jimmy. I explained what to expect the horse to do if he blew and I explained what *he* should do to counteract it, should that happen. I also told him that if he let go prematurely, I would kill him, if I didn't get killed first and if I got killed first, I would haunt him forever," she said matter-of-factly as Brandon snorted and started laughing again.

"Nothing like scaring the help!"

"My goal was to clarify my expectations! So, we have Wild Chuck tacked up. We're standing at the mounting block and I'm ready to throw a leg over him. The minute I put a foot in the stirrup and just before I swung my leg over, the horse blew, Jimmy panicked, jumped back like he'd seen big foot and let go. Wild Chuck took off like a bat out of hell across the arena, with me standing in one stirrup as he headed for the wall over there at a full gallop. Jimmy was screaming like a girl, the horse was upset and I was thinking I was about to become a bug splatter on the barn wall."

"What did you do?" Brandon managed to ask through his laughter.

"I pulled on the rein and pointed Wild Chuck's nose directly for the wall, knowing that he would happily run *along the wall* if he thought he could scrape me off but he would stop cold if he thought he was going to hit the wall first and thankfully he was smart enough to stop."

"Are there horses that aren't smart enough to stop?"

"Oh yea, we get them in here all the time!"

"Kate, were you OK?"

"I was OK and more importantly, the horse was OK," she said cautiously.

"Did you call it a day and get off?" Brandon asked, interested to see how tenacious she was.

"When Wild Chuck finally stopped running, I slowly swung my leg over his back and settled into the saddle for the first time, knowing that I had at least another 30 minutes of work ahead of me before we were finished. It was a long 30 minutes and most of that time was spent rebuilding his trust. The scariest part of the ride came after I was in the saddle."

"Did he buck?"

"No. Once I put both feet into the stirrups, Wild Chuck whipped his head around and looked at the toe of my boots, first the right and then the left."

"Why was that a big deal?"

"It was a big deal because his owner assured me that the trainer at the other barn had fully trained the horse and all he needed was a tune-up. When a horse whips his head around like that and looks at the toe of your boots in that way, what he's doing is trying to figure out what those are. In other words, that was the first time anyone had ever been on his back. I was thinking he was fresh when he bolted from Jimmy, but in fact, he was terrified because this was all new to him and his first experience under saddle and it was nearly my last."

"How did the rest of the ride go?"

"Once I realized he'd never been ridden before that moment, I changed my approach completely and it turned out OK. But poor Jimmy was mortified and it never happened again. There's something you should know about me Brandon," she said between bites, smiling at him.

"What's that?" he smirked with interest.

"My mother is a first-generation American who came to this country alone from Ireland when she was 20 years old. The Irish have a reputation for having a temper, as Jimmy found out that day!"

"I thought the Irish were known for being great fun?"

"If you mean, do we like to have a good time and are we fond of whiskey, the answer's yes, but as Shakespeare once said, we don't suffer fools!"

"Your mom is full Irish so that's where you got your auburn hair from?"

"Do you like the color?"

"Absolutely."

"Thanks." She hesitated for a moment before continuing, "I have a funny story to tell you about my hair. Before my mother died, she had beautiful auburn colored hair and of course, because she was Irish, it made sense, until I was in my teens and realized that the reason she went to the beauty shop every single Saturday, religiously, was to keep that color. She was actually a brunette! I'm also a brunette but to keep up my family's tradition, thanks to the hair dye companies, I have auburn colored hair," the pair shared a laugh.

Brandon became serious for a moment, "Kate, I understand that your mom has passed away. How old were you when that happened, if you don't mind my asking?

Katherine suddenly became somber, "It's Ok, I don't mind. I was 16 when it happened. I lost both my parents in a head-on collision with a drunk driver after they went out to dinner to celebrate their 20th wedding anniversary. The drunk survived and I lost both parents."

"Wow, I'm sorry Kate," he said sincerely reaching across the desk to take her hand.

"It was a long time ago..." she tried to be upbeat, staring at her food for a moment as he gently squeezed her hand.

"At the risk of prying and please, tell me if you think I am; what were they like?"

Her eyes drifted up from her plate as she studied him momentarily before smiling, "...I don't mind. They were the best. My mother was a teacher and my dad ran his own small company selling office products to local businesses. My mom lost a baby before I was born, so I ended up being an only child. It was great to be their kid." Katherine was staring at Brandon as she relayed the story, still holding hands.

"How did you get into horses?"

"My folks both rode, so I guess horses are in my blood. I was always fascinated by the emotional, well, almost spiritual relationship that you can have with a horse. As a little girl, my horse was my best friend and when my parents died, having horses saved my life. I don't know what I would've done if I didn't have horses in my life, especially during that time. Fox Ridge is my way of sharing that love with others so they can tap into the same level of fun and support that I had." She sat back, no longer holding hands, looking at Brandon.

"What is it?"

"Wow, I don't think I've ever said that to anyone before. You're very easy to talk to," Kate said honestly and a bit surprised at herself for opening up. While it scared her to reveal anything about her past, she had to admit that it felt good to talk about her parents and being with Brandon felt even better.

"Thanks, it's only because you're so interesting," he said casually, smiling between bites.

"You're a very good date. I've eaten like a pig and now, all I need is a good nap or a very long walk!"

"Then my work here is done. I had a great time too." Brandon smiled, their eyes locking for a long, silent moment.

"I'm looking forward to the banquet this weekend."

"Me too."

"I'd better clean up in here before we end our date."

"Let me help you with that," Brandon offered, moving around the desk coming close to her.

"Thanks," she smiled up at him. She could feel that flutter in her stomach again and while it was a new feeling for her, she was beginning to like it. Brandon was close enough to her that she could feel his breath on her neck and smell his aftershave. It gave her goose bumps. She turned to look at him, still holding her plastic fork and got plum sauce on his powder blue polo shirt.

"Brandon, I'm so sorry. Here, let me get that off!".

"It's Ok. It'll come out in the wash."

"No, I insist. Come with me." Without thinking, she took him by the hand and headed for the sink in her office. He followed her happily. Grabbing a clean towel from the counter top, Katherine got it wet and started to dab the stain on his chest. As she focused on her work, Brandon watched her intently. Noticing a piece of her hair that she had missed in her pony tail. He carefully took hold of the errant strand and tucked it behind her ear. They were very close. Katherine looked up slowly and for a brief moment, his gaze held hers. He desperately wanted to kiss her and so much more, but he could see that she was nervous, so instead, he caressed her upper arms, leaned in and whispered in her ear, "I had a good time tonight Kate."

"I did too," her voice cracked. She could feel that new excitement drumming deep in her core, enjoying his warm breath on her neck. She wondered if he could hear her heart pounding in her chest.

"I hope you aren't just saying that because you haven't been on a date in six years?" he smiled. Just then, there was a knock on the office door. Katherine stepped back as Jimmy entered.

"Well, I'd better leave you to it. I'm sure you have things to do before closing time. Kate, Jimmy, I'll see you at the banquet this weekend." With that, Brandon turned to Katherine and winked before heading for the office door.

"Brandon, thanks," she managed to say before he disappeared out the door.

CHAPTER 16: BANQUET NIGHT

It was 4:00pm, and the day of the annual awards banquet had finally arrived.

"Hey Girl, I almost called you a few minutes ago. I can't stand the suspense! Are you excited about tonight?"

"I'm looking forward to it. We worked like dogs for the past year and I think Fox Ridge is going to kick some butt tonight."

"Can you at least pretend to be a girl for just a minute and forget about the damned trophies and focus instead on the important part of the evening...*The Men*? Let me see what you look like! Hurry up, back away from the computer so I can get a full view."

"I really appreciate you sending me this dress. It's amazing," Katherine backed away from her laptop.

"Oh shit, you're beautiful. There won't be a man at the banquet who won't be drooling when they see you roll in wearing that. How do the shoes fit?" Sharon asked with both hands covering her mouth is awe.

"Not bad, I stuffed some toilet paper in the toes because they were a smidge too big, but they fit great now! It kind of reminded me of taking kids to horse shows where everyone borrows boots and stuffs the toes to make them fit."

"Tonight you're going to be a princess and if your prince charming is in that room, he's going to find you. In that dress, expect to be swarmed by men all night. I'm so excited for you. Your hair looks great too."

"It should, I have half a can of hair spray on it."

"Who did your make-up, it looks amazing?"

"Are you talking about the make-up on my face or on my arms?"

"On your arms?"

"Yeah, real horsewomen all have farmer tans where our short sleeved shirts cut across our biceps. I couldn't show up in a slinky gown with a farmer's tan, could I?"

"So, who did your face make-up?"

"Carl. You know, my fabulous Carl who has all the women flocking to him like kids in a candy shop!"

"God, he's amazing with make-up."

"Sadly, he made me promise not to tell anyone we know. He's afraid it'll ruin his playboy reputation with the ladies."

"I've got to meet him someday! When are you leaving for the event?"

"I'm driving Jimmy over in my truck, so as soon as he gets here, we're heading out."

"A farm truck is hardly the horse drawn carriage I had in mind for Cinderella, but I guess it'll have to do. Do you have the clutch?"

"No, my truck's an automatic."

Sharon laughed, "You twit! I'm not talking about a gear shift clutch, I'm talking about the small formal clutch that I included in the box with the dress."

"Oh, you mean the tiny purse? Why would anyone call that a clutch?"

"I don't know. Did you find it?"

"Yea, I found it and the jewelry. It all matches the dress really well so I look like I actually knew what I was doing when I got dressed! I'm so grateful that you thought of it. Otherwise, I would've shown up with my worn out leather purse, my wellies and no jewelry at all."

"Tonight, I feel like your Fairy Godmother. That clutch is just big enough to carry your cell phone, driver's license, some cash, lipstick and still have room for plenty of condoms," Sharon stated in a matter-of-fact tone. "You did get the condoms didn't you?"

"I couldn't buy condoms in this small town. I would've had to go out of town where no one knows who I am."

"You're not 16 years old for God's sake. Don't blame me when you want to bed someone at that banquet and you can't because you don't have any protection. Just don't say your Fairy Godmother didn't warn you," The duo started laughing.

"Somehow, I never pictured the Fairy Godmother chastising Cinderella for not picking up a box of Trojans before the ball. Oh, Jimmy's here. I'd love to stay and talk sex tips with my Fairy Godmother, but I've got to go."

"Kate, maybe Jimmy has some condoms?"

"I'm sure as hell not going to ask one of my employees if I can borrow a condom! What planet do you live on?"

"You can't technically borrow condoms and, by the way, you're going to need more than one. Make sure you tell Jimmy to shoot photos of you. I want to see how great you look at the event!"

"Ok. Anything for you. I can't thank you enough for everything you've done for me."

"It's just a dress Kate."

"No it isn't. You've been there for me since we were kids and I'm so grateful. I love you Sharon, you're the best friend a girl could ever hope for."

"I love you more. Cinderella, have a great time tonight and will you promise me just one thing?"

"Anything."

"Will you promise me that you'll be open to love tonight? At least until midnight? I'm not asking you to pick anyone up or to throw yourself at anyone. I'm just asking you to take down that wall around your heart until midnight and be open to love. Will you do that for me, just until midnight?"

Katherine sighed deeply, "…OK…I promise, as long as I don't have to do it longer than midnight."

"You won't need to. In that dress, love will find a way into your heart long before midnight!"

"Bye bye my Fairy Godmother," Katherine waved as she closed her laptop, hearing Jimmy knocking.

She hurried across the room to let him in. "Jimmy, you look very sharp. The girls are going to be flocking around you like bees to honey."

"Thanks, but I'm not looking for hook ups, I'm actually interested in someone."

"Could that be Brenda Ashford, by chance?"

"Yes, you could be right."

"Why didn't you invite her to join us tonight?" Katherine thought it was endearing that Jimmy blushed at the mere mention of her name.

"I don't think we're far enough along to go to a big banquet."

"Have you asked her out yet?"

"No, but I'm working up to it."

"If you need a Fairy Godmother to help move things along, I'd be happy to help."

Jimmy looked mortified by the suggestion, "No thanks. I'm just a good ole' cowboy from Texas and we don't rush these things. So, are you ready to go?"

"I just need to grab my purse and wrap and we'll be off. If you change your mind about needing a Fairy Godmother, let me know," Jimmy gasped as Katherine turned her back to him to grab her things from the nearby couch. "What's wrong?"

"That dress..." Jimmy's eyes resembled a deer in the headlights on a country road late at night.

"Don't you like it?"

"I like it very much. Is there a part that's missing?"

"Nope, this is all of it. What's the matter?"

"I'm worried about your safety in that dress!"

"I promise you, it won't fall off if that's what your worried about? Sarah hemmed it the other day so I won't trip over it." Katherine had a baffled look on her face.

"No, I'm worried that every man in the room is going to want to get near you in that dress."

"Jimmy, it's just a dress."

"No, it's not just a dress. That's the most amazing dress I've ever seen."

"Thanks. Then it's a good thing you and I are going together. If it turns out that you're right and I need protection, it'll be good to know you're with me."

"Don't worry, I'll protect you."

"Great! Then we'd better get going." Katherine walked past Jimmy heading for her truck while Jimmy stared at the back of that dress.

Ж

She and Jimmy drove nearly an hour to the venue. As they arrived, Jimmy exclaimed, "Wow, this place is gorgeous. Look at all those stairs leading up to the main door and the lights and that red carpet that goes all the way from the sidewalk to the top of the stairs. There's at least 30 stairs. This looks like one of those Hollywood movie premiers."

Holy shit, Katherine thought to herself when she realized she would have to climb all those stairs, quickly noting there were no handrails and she was wearing tissue stuffed stilts.

"Let's go win some trophies." Katherine tried to sound confident, cautiously walking around the front of the truck in the high heels. The valet watched the back of that dress with each step she took. The black satin flowed over her body like warm dark chocolate. Jimmy held out his arm to her on the sidewalk as she approached, seeing that she was not completely steady in the tall shoes.

"Thanks, don't mind if I do. The last thing I want is to face plant up those stairs or as I walk into the ballroom. I can't risk damaging this dress."

"That won't happen on my watch," Jimmy said proudly and the two headed for what seemed like a mountain of stairs leading up to the main entrance of the venue.

As they entered the building, Katherine draped her wrap over the arm carrying her clutch while hanging on to Jimmy's arm, just in case. *Geez, my feet hurt in these shoes already. Now I know how horses feel,* she thought as they slowly crossed the ballroom, heading for their assigned table. Heads were turning as every man in the room drank in that dress. The black satin fabric moved smoothly across every curve on her fit body. Katherine was grateful to finally arrive at the table without stumbling, completely clueless that she had caused such a stir. "Thanks for the escort."

"My pleasure. You know every guy in the room thinks you're my date and they're all envious of me right now," he whispered.

"You are my date. We came together. We're going to have dinner together and at the end of the evening we're going to leave together, so technically, you could be my date for the night."

"Wow, I guess you're right so all those guys should be envious of me tonight. Would you like a glass of wine?" he asked, noticing that each table had multiple bottles already open and waiting.

"Great idea. Between you, me and the fence post, I'm nervous as hell about the awards tonight and I could use a little courage in a bottle."

"You don't have a thing to worry about. Fox Ridge did really well this year and I'm sure we're going to take home several trophies," he poured two glasses of wine, sitting down at the table tasting the wine for the first time.

"You might just be my biggest fan. How do you like the wine?" Katherine remained standing, torn between her fear of wrinkling the dress if she sat down and her fear of falling off her shoes if she remained standing.

"Mmm, I didn't know wine tasted like this. It's very good, kind of like a grape Slurpee with lots of sugar in it."

Just then, Carl stopped by the table. "Oh, you look marveloussss. I saw that entrance you just made. Very slick that you crossed the room slowly so every man could drink you in, I love your make-up too."

"Why thanks, I had help with my make-up from someone really special. He does great work don't you think?"

Katherine leaned over to whisper in his ear, "That sexy, slow entrance was slow because I was afraid I would break my neck in these shoes." Carl snorted with laughter. "By the way, you look fabulous tonight!"

"I always look fabulous, just ask my harem," he smiled looking over to the table where their customers were just arriving. Carl was right, his tall, lean frame, draped in a gorgeous dark blue suit made him look like a model straight out of GQ. Katherine waved hello to the group of ladies.

"Can I talk to you for a moment?"

"What's up?"

"I'm worried about something."

"You can't be worried about the awards. We're going to kick butt tonight."

"No, that's not what I'm worried about..."

"What then?"

"Walking in these shoes!" With that, Carl howled with laughter.

"SHHH," she insisted, looking around to see if anyone could overhear them, leaning in close to him so she could whisper, caressing both of his biceps to avoid falling over.

"What's the matter with your shoes?" He whispered in her ear, trying to hold back his laughter, casually placing his hands on her hips to steady her as he looked around the room.

"Have you seen the height of these heels?" she asked while lifting her skirt up a few inches, exposing her foot.

"Katherine, those are called stilettos, are you afraid you'll look like a hooker wearing those shoes?"

"No, I'm terrified about climbing that flight of stairs over there to get to the stage. There's no railings to hang on to. Between the length of this gown and these shoes, I'm either going to break my neck, or I'm going to have to get on my knees and crawl. This being *a babe* stuff is harder than it looks."

"I expect we're going to win a lot of trophies tonight so we better figure out how to get you up there and back without a train wreck...I've got it. I'll walk you up and down the stairs!" Carl whispered triumphantly.

"God that would be great. Are you sure you don't mind?"

"Hell no. You know how I love the limelight."

"Solved! Of course, if we don't win anything, you won't need to babysit me, but if we do, I sure would appreciate the escort."

"Consider it done, and by the way, we're going to win a lot of trophies tonight. By my calculations, I count five for sure and maybe a sixth. I'll stick close to you until the awards are finished. After that, I'm going to attend to my harem. Deal?" He gently wrapped his arm around her waist.

"Deal. I don't want to crimp your style with the ladies," she whispered in his ear.

"Hey look, Dr. Baker is here with his posse," Carl announced, spotting the group even though the banquet hall was filling up. His height gave him a tremendous advantage over Katherine's shorter stature. She turned around to find Doctor Baker and his wife Mary approaching.

"Bob, great to see you and Mary, it's always a treat to spend an evening with you," Katherine smiled genuinely, leaning over to hug Bob and then Mary. Brandon was speechless. He couldn't believe how beautiful Katherine looked in her backless gown as he emerged from the crowded ballroom, approaching the table.

Katherine turned to the table, "You all know Dr. Baker and his wife Mary. Everyone exchanged hellos. Just then, Brandon and a beautiful brunette woman arrived at the table. Even though Katherine was thrown for a loop seeing Brandon with another woman, she couldn't argue with the way he looked, all dressed up in a black suit. His blue eyes and blonde hair looked amazing against his burgundy tie. She couldn't stop herself from staring as he approached.

"Brandon, I'm so glad you were able to come," Katherine said, leaning in to hug him.

Unable to put together a coherent sentence because he was so taken aback by how she looked, Brandon returned the hug, his fingertips accidentally touching her bare back. He suddenly felt like he was taking liberties and put his hands down by his sides.

"You've met Jennifer and Jimmy at the barn, but I don't think you've met Carl before," Carl extended his hand to Brandon.

"Carl, this is Dr. Brandon Stafford, he's taking over Bob's practice so Mary can see the world," Carl looked Brandon up and down as he shook his hand firmly.

"Good to meet you. I'm sure we'll get to know each other better in the months to come," Carl said, holding the hand shake a second longer than expected.

"I look forward to that. This is Stephanie Thomas...," Brandon said, but before he could finish his sentence, the P.A. kicked in and the announcer asked everyone to be seated, dinner was about to be served. Everyone said a quick hello to Stephanie as they all hustled back to their seats and the evening's festivities officially kicked off.

CHAPTER 17: THE DANCE

Stephanie was seated opposite Katherine at the very large round table so they didn't have a chance to speak during dinner. She thought Stephanie was strikingly beautiful, standing about 5'foot 7", thin with shoulder length blonde hair that was thick and gorgeous. She wore a fitted navy blue business suit and a cream colored satin camisole. After dinner, the plates were cleared, leaving only wine glasses and open bottles of wine as the award ceremony began. With each trip up to the podium, Brandon was struck by Katherine's beauty and that amazing backless dress. "Brandon, if you stare any harder at her, your eyes will pop out of your head," Stephanie remarked quietly as she gently elbowed him.

"Sis, she's really something isn't she?"

"I'm glad to see you're interested in someone. Since you got jilted by your fiancé, I hadn't seen you interested in anyone and I was starting to worry that you'd either given up on love or you were gay."

"You needn't worry. I was busy finishing school and trying to get my professional life started. I just didn't have time for a relationship and, just for the record, I'm not gay."

"But now that you're settled in your own practice, I'm glad to see you've got the hots for someone like Katherine. She seems really nice, she's certainly talented and you both like the same things," Stephanie said, squeezing Brandon's bicep lovingly, resting her head on his shoulder.

"I'm sorry to disappoint you Steph but I think she's already dating Carl."

"What gave you that idea?"

"Well, look at them. Every time she got up from the table, he was right there by her side and they're sitting next to each other. I think that says it all," Brandon remarked, the disappointment evident in his voice as Carl and Katherine returned to the table with yet another trophy. There would be six on the table before the ceremonies were finished and with each win, the customer table erupted with applause. Katherine gave a short acceptance speech each time thanking her customers and staff before returning to the table, escorted by Carl.

Soon after the final award was presented, the band kicked in and people started to dance. Dr. Baker invited Mary onto the dance floor while Carl leaned over to speak to Katherine.

"Are you going to be Ok if I visit with my ladies at our other table?" He whispered in her ear.

"I'll be fine now. I owe you one for saving my ass tonight," Katherine whispered and the two shared a private laugh as he got up to leave the table. Before he left, he gently moved a piece of her hair back onto the hair pin that had come loose. What they didn't know was that Brandon was watching them.

A few minutes later, Katherine decided to take her chances flying solo and headed for the bar. While there was plenty of wine at the table, what she really wanted was a good stiff scotch both to calm her nerves and to celebrate. As she neared the bar she was intercepted by Hadley Vinton, owner of Vinton Farms. Hadley was her biggest competitor and the one person in the room who would've won all six of those trophies if Katherine wasn't in his way. Hadley wore a dark brown suit with a dress shirt whose buttons were groaning under the pressure of his rotund belly.

Brandon excused himself from the table. As he neared Katherine, he couldn't help but overhear the heated conversation in hushed tones between the two barn owners.

"...Katie, if you steal one more of my customers, I'm going to destroy you," Hadley warned in a firm voice while getting in Katherine's face. A large, gray haired, pot-bellied man, Hadley celebrated his 65th birthday that year. Although it had been decades since he was on a horse, Hadley was a great businessman and Vinton Farms was doing very well as a result. Katherine looked like a child standing next to him. Vinton Farms took home a total of three trophies and while any normal barn owner would've been thrilled, Hadley Vinton was furious, blaming Katherine for his loss of the other six.

She smiled, getting in Hadley's face, or as close as she could while he towered over her. She quietly stated to him in a calm voice, "Hadley, you son of a bitch, if you treated your customers better, they wouldn't be calling me and you know it." At first Brandon was concerned that Katherine might need some help but he stopped in his tracks when he realized she had things well in hand.

"You know I like you, but you drink too much, and you can't keep your hands off your female clients. You don't need me to steal your customers, they're going to leave you if you keep acting like a horse's ass. Why don't you let me buy you a ginger ale so you can sober up while I get myself a double scotch?"

Hadley laughed out loud. "It's a free bar Katie and you're the only woman I know who could drink a man under the table and do it with scotch. However, in that dress, I'd agree to anything you wanted."

"As my mother used to say, it's my Irish heritage that accounts for my thirst."

"And for your temper," he added. Katherine took Hadley by the arm and the pair headed over to the bar for their drinks.

"Can I get one ginger-ale on ice and a double scotch, neat please?" Katherine asked the bartender, smiling.

"Yes mam," he quickly poured the two drinks and placed the ginger-ale in front of her and the scotch in front of Hadley.

"Excuse me, the scotch is mine," she pointed out to the bartender.

"Yes mam" he jumped, his voice beaming with surprise and respect as he switched the drinks.

The pair picked up their drinks, Katherine clinked their glasses together and toasted, "To healthy competition. May the best son of a bitch win."

"If we're competing to see who's the best son of a bitch, you're going to win hands down on that one," Hadley laughed as the two took a sip from their drinks.

"You know I'd love to get insulted by you all night long but I need to get back to MY customers."

"You mean you need to get back to MY customers, don't you?"

"If I wanted to take your customers, I could. Fortunately I don't have to go to all that trouble because you're driving them to me and I appreciate your support. Enjoy your evening Hadley," and with that, she patted him on the arm. The two rivals laughed, and she was off to make the solo trip back to her table, double scotch in hand. Hadley watched her slowly walk away, studying her in that amazing dress.

As she had traveled only a few steps, she spotted Brandon for the first time. "Well, hello, are you enjoying yourself?" she asked, a bit surprised to find him staring at her.

"Yes, clearly more than he is."

"What do you mean?"

"I was a little worried about you back there and almost stepped in to rescue you until I heard you call that man a son of a bitch and then I realized you didn't need any help from anybody, so I stayed out of it."

"Why Dr. Stafford, I like the thought of you being my knight in shining armor ready to swoop in to save *Katherine the Great*. Luckily you didn't need to save me tonight. Do you want a drink while we're here?"

"Absolutely. Can I get a beer?" Brandon called out to the man behind the bar.

"Sure thing." Brandon stepped over to the bar to get his beer before coming back to Katherine. "Do you want me to freshen up your scotch, mam?"

"No thanks, I'm good."

"Let's get back to our table and enjoy the evening." Although she was sorely disappointed that he had a date with him, Katherine was still grateful for an arm to hang onto.

"May I have the honor of this dance?" Dr. Baker asked, extending his hand to Katherine as she approached the table.

"I would love to!" Katherine took a sip of her double scotch before setting it down on the table and heading to the dance floor for a slow song.

Dr. Baker looked especially distinguished in his brown tweed jacket, matching tie and dark trousers. While the couple enjoyed the music, Dr. Baker remarked, "Kate, you know, Brandon has a little crush on you."

Katherine snorted with unbridled laughter, "You must be going senile, he has a date tonight or didn't you notice?"

Bob laughed, "Stephanie isn't Brandon's date."

"She isn't? If she's not his date, is she yours? You and I both know Mary's gonna skin you alive if she finds out you're dating around," she giggled as the couple moved across the dance floor.

"Stephanie is Brandon's sister. She's in town for a business meeting and he invited her to come to the banquet. And, by the way, the only thing Brandon could talk about yesterday was his dinner at the barn the night before and the amazing banana bread you baked for him. That's how I know he has a little crush on you," Katherine blushed, feeling both embarrassed at her mistaking Brandon's sister for his date as well as excitement at the thought that Brandon had a crush on her.

"Wow, do I feel like a knucklehead now." Glancing over to the table, she noticed Brandon staring at them. She smiled and mentioned, "You know, this may be the last time you and I get to dance together. I'm going to miss you and Mary more than you know."

"Brother of mine, you should go ask Katherine to dance."

"I can't do that, she's here with a date. You know how long I've been out of the dating scene but we had dinner together the other night and she didn't even mention Carl. She said she didn't have time for a man in her life. I guess I don't understand dating today."

"From everything Bob and Mary have said about her, Katherine doesn't strike me as the kind of woman who plays men. It won't hurt to have a dance. Bob's dancing with her and Carl doesn't seem to care one bit. In fact, he's over at the other table flirting with all those ladies. Go on, ask her!"

"Well, I guess you're right, one dance can't hurt."

A moment later Dr. Baker felt a tap on his shoulder and turned around to see it was Brandon.

"May I cut in?"

"Bob, do you mind?"

"No. I can see I'm already being replaced around here," The trio laughed politely as they switched partners.

"Well then, Dr. Stafford, I would love to dance with you, she replied taking his hand as he enveloped her gently in his arms.

Brandon moved his right hand to her back. Excited to finally touch the soft skin that he'd been lusting after all night long. As he drew her in slowly, he asked, "Katherine, is Carl going to be upset that we're dancing together?"

"Please call me Kate and no, Carl won't mind if we dance together, why do you ask?"

"I thought he was your date for the evening?"

"Really?" A look of confusion came over her face.

"Yea. He was eyeing me when you introduced us, so I assumed he was being protective or territorial because he was your date for the evening. Every time you won an award, he went with you and before he left to go to the other table, he touched your hair, so I figured you were in a relation-ship." Confusion now written all over his face.

Katherine laughed and whispered in his ear, "Can I tell you a secret?"

"Sure," he leaned into her, enjoying the closeness.

"But you have to swear not to tell anyone. OK?"

"Ok, I swear."

She leaned in so her mouth was close to his ear and whispered, "Carl only stuck close to me tonight because I was afraid I would fall off these shoes! You saw him touch my hair because he's anal about the details. You should see him prepping horses for the show ring. He's so detail oriented that he makes Martha Stewart look like a slacker. Tonight, he was looking at me like I was another show horse going into the ring!"

"What?" he laughed, his hand now comfortably caressing her back, his fingertips slipping under the fabric along her rib cage. "Is that why he's over at the client table flirting with all the women in their ball gowns?" Brandon whispered in her ear as he gently guided Katherine around the dance floor.

"That good ole' boy is a legendary flirt. Now, remember, you swore not to breathe a word of this to anyone." She whispered. Katherine wanted to tell Brandon that Carl was gay, but it wasn't her place to divulge Carl's secret and if anyone knew the importance of keeping secrets, she did.

"I swear, I won't say a word. Does that mean you're not dating anyone?" Brandon gazed into her eyes.

"I'm not dating anyone. Our dinner date was the first 'date' I've been on since I arrived here six years ago. I would never have accepted your invitation if I were dating someone. The truth of the matter is that I rarely have time to date and frankly, as you witnessed with Hadley, I'm not really considered ideal dating material anyway," she smiled, looking away for a moment, a hint of sadness in her tone.

Gently pulling her closer to him, "Don't sell yourself short. You're smart, talented, independent and frankly, I think you've just been dating the wrong men," Brandon suggested, as his fingertips explored her bare back, enjoying her warm, soft skin.

Katherine gasped softly, savoring his touch. "Are you dating anyone now?"

"No, I've been too busy with school, then with finding a practice and moving, so I haven't been on a date in years. I wouldn't have asked you out to dinner if I were dating someone. I wasn't raised that way."

Katherine arched her back slightly at his touch, his embrace gently drawing her in closer. She tenderly closed her hand around his and let the fingers of her left hand explore his shoulder and back. The pair was quiet for a few moments before Katherine rested her head against his shoulder and closed her eyes, enjoying the feeling of being safely enveloped in his strong arms. Brandon leaned his head gently against hers. The first slow song ended and the pair didn't even notice.

"Kate, what's that scent you're wearing?"

"It's called, 'half a bottle of hair spray,'" she giggled honestly, somewhat embarrassed but grateful that she didn't smell like horse from the drive over in the farm truck.

"Well, whatever it is, you smell great."

"Thanks. You look very handsome tonight," she replied, snuggling close to him as they slow danced. There were feelings stirring deep in her core that she'd never felt before with any other man. While she didn't fully understand them, she knew she wanted more.

Katherine remembered her promise to Sharon, she would be open to love tonight but only for tonight. At the end of the evening, like Cinderella, she'd go back to her normal life of seclusion and secrecy. But for tonight, she would lower her guard and give love a chance. Glancing at her watch, *It's only 7:00 so love, you still have five hours to work your magic,* she thought to herself, excited for the first time to see where it might lead.

They were lost in each other's arms until Brandon brought his lips close to her ear. "Kate, have I told you look beautiful this evening?" he whispered. She was as excited by the feeling of his breath upon her ear as she was by his words.

Feeling a bit awkward at his compliment, Katherine tried to make a joke, "Mmmm, why, Dr. Stafford, are you flirting with me?" She whispered back, slowly looking him in the eye.

"I'm trying, but I must admit I'm very rusty at this." Brandon leaned his lips closer to her ear and whispered, "Maybe...I should ask Carl for some pointers." Katherine snorted loudly and the pair broke out in laughter, still in each other's arms before suddenly realizing there was no music playing and the band was gone. The band apparently left at some point to go on a break and they hadn't noticed. The duo quickly returned to the table hand-in-hand, a bit embarrassed but in good spirits.

"Katherine would you like to dance?" Jimmy asked loudly, barely able to stand. The people at the table found his behavior very funny because Jimmy never drank. However, tonight, he'd started drinking before dinner and hadn't stopped until he emptied the last of the wine bottles on the table.

Shocked to see Jimmy drunk for the first time, "I think you've danced your last dance for the evening. It's time for me to take you home my friend," While he was acting very funny, she felt sorry for him, knowing the kind of hangover that would come from that much wine.

"I'm celebrating all our trophies. You did a great job this year and we should all celebrate. Here, have some of this grape juice, it's almost as good as a cherry Slurpee!"

"Katherine, would you like us to bring him home?" Doctor Baker generously offered.

"Thanks, but I brought Jimmy tonight and as his surrogate mom, I need to take my child home." Saddened to realize that the promise she'd made to Sharon was now officially shot to hell. "Well, good night everyone." *This is just my luck. The one and only time I'm dressed up, I don't smell like horse shit and I promise to be open to love, I end up driving Jimmy home. Odds are, the most memorable moment of this evening will probably include him puking on me on the way back to the farm. The universe surely does have a twisted sense of humor,* she thought to herself.

Brandon was equally disappointed to see the evening come to an abrupt end. Stephanie leaned over to her brother, "Brandon, it would be the gentlemanly thing to offer Katherine a hand."

"I don't want to scare her off by offering to go home with her and besides, you're my guest tonight. I can't leave you."

"As a woman myself, I can assure you, you won't scare her off. I'm sure Bob and Mary can entertain me," Stephanie smiled, squeezing his arm. She leaned over to Mary for a moment. "Mary, would you mind me staying behind if Brandon escorts Katherine back to her farm?"

"We'd be delighted to spend the evening with you," Mary said winking mischievously.

"There you have it. It's all settled. Now go, do the gentlemanly thing!"

As Katherine picked up her wrap and clutch, she heard Brandon offer, "Katherine, may I give you a hand? Stephanie's going to stay with Bob and Mary and I can ride with you, if you'd like," he offered tentatively.

Delighted by the offer, she could feel her face getting hot, "I hate to bother you and I hate to cut your evening short, but I could use a hand. If you don't mind."

"I'm happy to do it...Bob, when you're ready to go home, could you swing by Fox Ridge to pick me up?"

"Sure."

"Stephanie, are you sure you don't mind?" Katherine asked seriously.

"Not at all. Bob and Mary will entertain me so you two can take care of Jimmy."

"Thanks. Good night everybody. Come on Jimmy, I think you've had more than enough fun for one evening," Katherine put his arm around her neck as Brandon supported him from the other side.

"Carl, would you mind gathering up our trophies and bringing them to the barn tomorrow?" Katherine called over to the customer's table where Carl was busy flirting.

"Will do. Are you heading home already?"

"Yes, Jimmy's ready to go."

"Ok, have a good evening and congratulations on everything. It looks like you're the big winner for the night!" He called over with an impish grin on his face.

"Everyone from Fox Ridge is a big winner for the night!" With that, Carl's table filled with the clients from Fox Ridge erupted in applause.

CHAPTER 18: JIMMY'S BIG NIGHT

T he trio headed down the stairs in the front of the building where they waited for the valet to bring the truck around. Katherine wasn't sure who was going to fall down the long staircase first, drunken Jimmy or stiletto-challenged Katherine. Thankfully, both managed to stay on their feet with Brandon's help.

"I'll pour him into the back seat."

"Thanks. I'd appreciate that. I can't imagine how ladylike I would look in this outfit dragging Jimmy into the back of my truck like a sack of feed." Kate watched as Brandon carefully assisted Jimmy into the back seat where he stretched out and quickly passed out. Jimmy's small stature was no match for Brandon's six foot frame.

"Shall I drive?"

Katherine found herself speechless for a moment, "That's very gallant of you. Thanks, that would be lovely," Katherine answered coyly, grateful that she didn't have to step off the sidewalk and maneuver around to the driver's side door. The added bonus was that the truck was parked close to the curb on the passenger's side so she essentially had a mounting block. *I've been damn lucky tonight that I haven't landed on my ass in these shoes. Why in the hell would anyone wear these things?* She wondered.

"Allow me," Brandon offered, opening the passenger's side door for

Kate. She was suddenly mortified, knowing there was no ladylike way to get into a truck with heels as high as these. Even though she had the curb as her mounting block, the truck had grated steel running boards which almost guaranteed she would put a heel through one of the holes on her way in, trapping her foot like a wild animal in a snare.

"I'm warning you, this isn't going to be pretty to watch," her face turning red as the valets, trying hard to be inconspicuous watched intently.

"Happy to give you a leg-up if you need one," Brandon suggested calmly as he chuckled, their eyes meeting for one humorous, yet terribly awkward moment.

"I've got a better idea, may I?" she placed her hand on his shoulder and took off her high heels, setting them delicately onto the front seat. She was careful to make sure the tissue paper she'd stuff into the toes didn't fall out in the process. "I know how to get into a truck this way," she laughed and lifted her skirt just enough to be able to step up onto the running boards and hop easily into the truck. Brandon smiled as he watched her bare back slip into her seat, as did the valets. He closed the door behind her and headed over to driver's side. "I hope you don't mind but I'll need to adjust the seat. My legs are a bit longer than yours."

"No worries. Bob suggested recently that in some circles I could be considered a 'little person.' While I always thought of myself as tall, I guess I might be considered short by some standards." Katherine smiled focusing her attention on buckling her seatbelt without wrinkling the dress in the process. Jimmy was already sacked out in the back seat and he soon started to snore, leaving Katherine and Brandon an opportunity to get to know each other better for the hour-long drive back to Fox Ridge.

"If I haven't already said so, thanks for coming home with me tonight. I really appreciate the help." She said honestly gently squeezing his arm.

"You're welcome. I was going to offer earlier but I was concerned that you might be creeped out by a man you barely know, offering to come home with you. Stephanie actually told me you wouldn't think I was a stalker and encouraged me to offer."

"Oh crap, I never thought about the stalker thing. You're not a stalker are you?" She laughed.

"No, you'll always be safe with me. My mother raised me to be a gentleman."

"Please thank your mother for me! So, why did you choose North Carolina to start your practice?" Kate asked as he pulled out of the parking lot and headed down the highway. It was a beautiful, cloudless fall evening. The full moon illuminated the otherwise dark country highway for their drive back to the farm. She was eager to get to know more about this handsome, kind hearted man who had her experiencing feelings she'd never had before.

"I was raised on our family's dairy farm in Wisconsin and hadn't traveled much in my life so when Bob's business came on the market, it seemed like a great adventure. When I met he and Mary, well, that sealed the deal. I knew this was the perfect fit for me. How about you? Why did you relocate to North Carolina?" he asked, periodically glancing at Katherine while spending most of his time watching the road.

"I was looking for a fresh start...So, did you enjoy college?" Katherine masterfully diverted the conversation.

"Yea, I loved it. I got into sports and did a bit of partying. It was all such a change from the farm."

"Bob mentioned that you postponed vet school so you could help your family?"

"I did. My parents were getting older and I decided to postpone vet school to help them for as long as I could. They've since retired and sold the farm, so it all worked out fine."

"That was nice of you to do that. Do they still live in Wisconsin?" she four herself studying him. *Geez, he's a nice guy*, she thought to herself.

"They'll never leave Wisconsin. The rest of our family still lives up there so it's handy for my folks. My younger sister Stephanie, who you met tonight, lives about 30 minutes from my folks with her husband and there are aunts, uncles, grandparents, you know, the usual large family."

"That was funny tonight at the banquet, I thought Stephanie was your date until Bob told me on the dance floor that she was your sister."

"That's crazy because I said the same thing to Steph about you and Carl." The two laughed over how silly their misunderstanding had been. Before they could say anything else, Jimmy started to moan in the back seat.

"Oh shit! I think we'd better pull over. Jimmy sounds like he's gonna be sick," Katherine warned, looking into the back seat.

"Will do," Brandon quickly pulled off the highway into a deserted parking lot.

"Kate, why don't you stay in the truck, I've got this."

"Are you sure you don't want any help?"

"I'm sure. This isn't my first rodeo," Brandon laughed. The trio spent the next 20 minutes in the parking lot while Jimmy puked his guts out as only an inexperienced wine drinker can. Katherine watched, passenger side doors both wide open, her bare feet resting on the running boards as Brandon supported Jimmy while he heaved into the grass at the edge of the parking lot. When they were fairly certain he'd thrown up everything short of the kitchen sink, Brandon helped him back into the truck and they resumed their journey.

Soon, Katherine could once again hear Jimmy snoring in the back seat. She was grateful, knowing that as long as he was asleep, the chances of him throwing up on her or the truck were minimal.

"Thanks for what you did back there."

"No problem. We've all been in that situation at one time or another." He glanced over at her with a knowing smile.

"So, what kind of sports did you play in college?"

"I wanted to play football but I didn't make the team. A friend suggested I check out boxing. I fell in love with that."

"You did? Isn't that all about blood and guts and missing teeth and broken faces?"

"If it's done right, it's all about strategy and out thinking your opponent and using your reflexes to avoid getting hit. It's a lot more of a mental sport than people might think. There's a lot of physics involved to maximize your punches with the least amount of effort and energy expended. I really liked it."

"That sounds a lot like horse training. How did you do?"

"We were State Champions and I was singled out as MVP for two out of the four years. All in all, I'd say, I did Ok." He smiled, glancing over at her.

"Remind me to never get on your bad side. Do you ride?"

"Yea, but nothing like you do. We always had horses on the farm. We used them for moving the larger herds of cattle but mostly for fun. Stephanie and I would ride bareback into the pond and dive off the backs of our horses. Of course, we didn't do that in the cow ponds. We had a separate pond for swimming. Thank God or I wouldn't have survived my childhood. Have you ever seen what a cow pond looks like? It's like a giant green Petri dish."

Katherine snorted with laughter. She thought to herself, *Oh my God, he's not only cute and helpful and a vet, but he's really funny too.*

Brandon took on a more serious tone for a moment, "Kate, if you don't mind my asking, after your parents passed away, where did you go?"

"I come from a very small family but my mother had an older sister in New York and I went to live with her."

"For how long?"

"I'll be the first to admit, I wasn't easy to live with after losing both my parents. My aunt should've gotten a medal for putting up with an angry 16-year-old who was desperate to build a family to replace the one she'd lost. I'm afraid all that stress may have been part of the reason she passed away a few years later," she bemoaned, the regret permeating her answer.

Katherine turned to look at him, "Brandon, thanks for our dance tonight. It was special and it's a memory I'll cherish," she said, their eyes met for a moment.

"I enjoyed it too. I'm just sorry we had to cut the evening short. There'll be plenty of opportunities in the future to go out dancing."

Katherine smiled at Brandon before turning to look into the darkness outside the passenger window. *If I take the job in Canada, there won't be any more dances with Brandon,* she thought to herself. Katherine hadn't told anyone but Dr. Baker about the job offer. This was just one more secret she was carrying alone. *I'm not going to think about the Canadian job tonight. I'm just going to focus on letting down my walls like I promised Sharon I would and we'll see what happens,* she resolved.

The couple continued to share lively conversation with the steady sound of Jimmy's snoring in the backseat as their background music. It seemed like only a few minutes before they were heading into the driveway at Fox Ridge Equestrian Center. "Gee, even with the extra stop for Jimmy's puking, I can't believe we're here so fast," Katherine declared as Brandon drove over the familiar cattle guard at the entrance to the long driveway.

"Did you leave your house lights on?"

"Sarah's probably in the house. She's in charge of the barn tonight. Actually, we're home much earlier than she probably expected us to be."

As they pulled up to the house, Sarah came out onto the front patio to greet them. "Hi Katherine, I thought you drove to the banquet with Jimmy? Hi Dr. Stafford. Did Jimmy get lucky and leave you behind?"

"Hi Sarah," Brandon replied as he stepped out of the truck.

"I did drive to the banquet with Jimmy. No, he didn't get lucky, but he did get a bit sloshed at the event so Dr. Stafford was nice enough to offer to help me bring him home. I'm going to have Jimmy sleep it off on my couch," she replied while stepping out of the truck carefully carrying her shoes in her hand.

"My poor sweet Jimmy. What the heck was he thinking?"

"I think there was some confusion over the wine. He thought it was grape juice and liked it a bit too much. You know how he loves his cherry Slurpee's. He's passed out in the back seat of the truck," Katherine said, opening the back door on the passenger's side.

"I'll get him Kate," Brandon offered as he came around the front of the truck. Katherine was already leaning into the back seat to see if Jimmy was awake.

"I'm afraid he's out of it," Brandon gently leaned over her, one hand on the top of the door frame and the other gently stroking her bare back.

"Ohhh," she exhaled her approval. Luckily the truck door blocked Sarah's view.

"Brandon..," Kate purred.

"Sorry Kate," he whispered apologetically, "That dress is driving me crazy."

"Don't be sorry, I've been told it was designed to do that," she whispered with a smile.

"I'd better get Jimmy inside."

"Thanks," Katherine turned to move out of the way. The two were now face-to-face wedged between the open truck door and the back seat. Katherine hesitated, placing her hand on Brandon's chest as he leaned in softly to kiss her. That familiar stirring deep within was back. She wanted to kiss him badly but quickly came to her senses and slid out of the way so Brandon could reach Jimmy. The last thing she wanted was for a member of her staff to catch her kissing anyone.

"I'll get a pillow and some blankets for the couch. Do you want some help bringing him in?" Katherine asked, grabbing her wrap, clutch and shoes before rushing for the front door.

"No thanks, I can manage," Brandon gently pulled Jimmy out of the back seat and draped him over his shoulder to carry him into the house like a sack of grain. He had to duck coming in the front door to ensure he didn't bang Jimmy into the door frame. By the time he entered the house, the bedding was already on the couch.

"You're welcome to put him there for the night. I'll get him a bath towel, a trash can and a bottle of water, just in case he needs them," Katherine headed back into the bedroom with bare feet to collect the first two items. Although Brandon was busy with Jimmy, he couldn't help but notice how the black satin flowed like water over every curve as she moved across the room.

Brandon snapped back into reality when Sarah mused sympathetically, "Good idea. Poor, Poor Jimmy, you're going to be hurting big time in the morning."

"Sarah, Is the barn closed up for the night already?"

"Yep, everyone is snug in their beds. I did the final walk-thru about 10 minutes before you drove in."

"Then, while this is going to be one of Jimmy's worst nights, it's your lucky night because we're back early so you can head home if you want," Katherine offered.

"That's great. Whoo hoo, I get to spend a quiet evening at home with my husband because the kids will be on their way to bed already," Sarah delighted. "By the way, the dress turned out great! How did the awards go?" She asked a bit cautiously. "Did we win anything?"

"We won six out of ten. I'd say it was a good evening. Oh, and by all accounts, the dress was a big hit." Katherine couldn't help but notice that Brandon was smiling at her from across the room.

"I didn't see any trophies so I was afraid to ask."

"Oh, Carl's bringing the trophies tomorrow. I was a little worried that if Jimmy got sick in the truck, well you know." The trio laughed.

"Dr. Stafford, do you need a lift home?" Sarah offered politely.

"No, but thanks for asking. Dr. Baker's going to pick me up on his way back from the banquet."

"Great, then I'll say good-night and call my hubby from my car."

"Thanks again for your help with this dress. I'll see you on Monday morning."

"You're welcome! Good night," Sarah replied as she headed out the door.

"Good night," Brandon called out as Katherine closed the door behind Sarah.

"Would you like some coffee? Or... maybe you'd prefer a brandy?" Katherine suggested enthusiastically with the same mischievous excitement you would expect from a high schooler who just discovered their parent's liquor cabinet for the first time.

"You have brandy?"

"One of my customers gave me a really good bottle during the holidays. I haven't even opened it yet, however, if you're game, I'm game," she smiled wickedly.

"Let's do it!"

"I'm afraid I don't have proper brandy snifters but will a regular glass do?"

"Kate, I would happily sip good brandy out of a cereal bowl if that's all you had."

"Well then, you'll be very happy because I can offer you a clean drinking glass instead."

"Brilliant," Katherine bent over, opening the lower cabinet in the living room to pull out the coveted bottle of brandy. Brandon found himself staring once again, wondering what it would be like to make love to her. To hear her moan his name as she orgasmed beneath him.

Unaware of this, Katherine stood up and turned to hand the bottle to Brandon. "What's the matter?"

"It's that dress."

"Oh, is that all. Brandon, it's just a dress," she laughed, certain he had to be joking. Katherine was oblivious to the impact it was having on Brandon. *I'll have to tell Sharon this dress has magical powers when I skype with her tomorrow,* she thought.

"No Kate, it isn't just a dress," He remarked sincerely. She suddenly felt nervous excitement, realizing he wasn't kidding after all.

"Here, if you'll open the bottle, I'll round us up some glasses," she handed the bottle to him moving into the snug but serviceable kitchen in her bare feet. Brandon followed her.

"I had a good time tonight. How about you?"

"Considering we won six out of ten trophies, I didn't break my neck in those shoes, I got to dance with you and Jimmy didn't puke on me or in my truck, I'd say it was a fabulous evening. And, I owe you one," she took the open bottle from him, pouring two glasses of brandy.

"It was my pleasure," Brandon moved close to her in the tiny kitchen. As she turned to hand him a glass, he leaned in, placing his hands on either side of her, pressing her gently against the counter. She set the glass down on the counter. Her heart was beating out of her chest. His eyes were dark and filled with desire. Brandon lowered his head slowly until his lips were inches away from hers. "Kate, I'd like to kiss you." He whispered.

"You would?" she whispered.

"I would," he lowered his head, his lips brushing against hers. They were soft and tender. For the first time in her life, she wanted a man. She wanted to taste him, to kiss him, to make love with him.

Her head was swimming in a way she'd never experienced before. The smell of his aftershave was overwhelming. She managed to rest her hands against his firm chest, her lips reaching up to meet his in a kiss that sent shockwaves throughout her body in all He drew her into him. One hand exploring her bare back while the other moved up behind her head, holding it in the perfect position for his lips to explore her mouth, her neck and beyond. Her breathing was fast and hard, filled with heat and a need she never realized existed before that moment.

Brandon wanted to make love with her right there in the small kitchen but with Jimmy asleep not 15 feet away, he decided he'd have to wait. Instead, he kissed her one final time and smiled to find that her eyes were still closed. He released her from his embrace, before picking up both glasses, handing one to her and whispered, "Cheers to a great evening and congratulations on all the trophies."

Katherine was speechless for a moment, still reeling from the intensity of his kisses. She finally managed to whisper, "Thanks...to a great evening," and then took a large gulp of her brandy. It made her cough. Brandon smiled, knowing that she was aroused and rattled at the same time. She found herself drawn to him and the more time she spent around him, the more she wanted him. Katherine knew just how dangerous it was for her to get involved with anyone but in the battle between her head and her heart, tonight, her heart was the victor.

"Oh my God that's good," she exclaimed with one more cough.

"The brandy or the kiss?"

"...Both..." Brandon was pleased to see just how rattled she was.

"I'd better check on Jimmy," Brandon moved back so she could pass. In addition to wanting to check on Jimmy, Katherine really wanted to get out of the close quarters of her kitchen before things got out of hand. In the open floor plan of her modest ranch style home, the kitchen lights were still on, illuminating the dining room and living room with a soft glow.

As Katherine finished tucking Jimmy in, she headed back toward the kitchen where Brandon was leaning his hip against the counter, sipping his brandy, watching her. "Since our evening was cut short and we're both dressed up with nowhere to go, as the saying goes, would you care to dance?"

Katherine hesitated, but her excitement over spending the evening with this wonderful man overruled her many concerns, "I would...love to. Let me turn on some music," she smiled, taking one more sip of her drink before setting it down to address the stereo. Brandon couldn't wait to get his arms around her again.

Katherine turned on an easy listening station that was playing romantic tunes from the 80's. She took one more gulp of brandy before she approached Brandon. His left hand extended to take hers.

"Have I told you how lovely you look tonight?" he whispered in her ear while his right arm tenderly enveloped her back, gently but decidedly drawing her close. His lips brushing against her neck.

"Mmmm," she exhaled softly, "Yes, I think you did but feel free to say it as often as you like," she whispered, leaning her head away, exposing her neck to his lips. The couple danced in the soft glow from the kitchen, with Jimmy's snoring in the background. The fingertips of her left hand, gently stroking his hair.

"That's nice..." he whispered, his hand continuing his exploration of her bare back through the first and second songs. She felt safe in his strong arms. Her heart beating fast and hard with excitement. His left hand engulfed her tiny hand. He brought both close to his chest. His mouth continued to enjoy the taste of her throat, her ear lobe, both of which were turning her on. Their exploration was silent and purely physical as the music played on. She could feel his hardness against her belly, making her want him even more. Her left hand slipped down his shoulder slowly to caress his strong bicep. She rested her head against his chest and closed her eyes, swept away by the music and his kisses. For the first time in her life, she felt equal measures of safety and an intense desire to make love with this man. At the end of the third song, Brandon stopped for a moment. Katherine looked up, meeting his gaze. His eyes dark, he drew her body tightly to his. He lowered his head to kiss her again. Katherine felt a flutter in her stomach that was new and she wanted more. As his lips neared hers, she rocked her head back and closed her eyes in happy surrender. It was clear to her that Brandon wanted to sleep with her and at that moment, she would've agreed to anything he asked of her. She could feel his lips close to hers...just as his cell phone rang.

"Ohhh," she gasped, quickly stepping away from his embrace, acting like a child who was caught with their hand in the cookie jar.

"Great timing," Brandon bemoaned quietly, the disappointment in his voice obvious as he pulled his phone from his jacket pocket.

"Dr. Stafford," he answered with a facetious smile on his face. "...Ok. See you then."

"Was that Bob?" Katherine asked nervously, picking up her brandy and finishing it off with one large gulp.

"Yes, he's turning into the driveway right now," Katherine choked on her drink, surprised that Bob was already on the property.

"Damn!"

"Kate, this was the best evening I can remember in many years," he said sincerely, taking her by the hand, looking deep into her eyes.

"Me too," she smiled, nervously glancing out the front window watching for headlights. Not only was she surprised that Bob was on the property but she was equally surprised that she nearly let herself sleep with Brandon, knowing how dangerous that could be. The fact that she was so comfortable around this man and so sexually attracted to him scared her to death.

A moment later she spotted Bob's headlights coming up the drive. Katherine pulled her hand away from Brandon's and exclaimed nervously, "Oh look, there's Bob!" surprised by how fast he'd gotten up the long driveway. "Yikes, I need to get outside so he doesn't think we've been fooling around," she dashed for the front door.

"You're funny. What if they'd found us kissing?" He asked curiously, still standing in the same spot.

"What! Brandon, it's a small town and I'm a single woman. I'm paranoid about not giving the impression that I'm loose."

"Is *Katherine the Great* loose?" Brandon chuckled.

"Of course not," she countered with a giggle. "But I don't want people to get the idea that I might be. Ok, I admit it, I'm paranoid. But I take my responsibilities very seriously and I don't want parents to ever worry about leaving their children in the hands of a loose woman," They both laughed as she opened the front door and stepped carefully out onto the patio in her bare feet, waving to the approaching vehicle.

"They wouldn't think you were loose if they'd found us kissing," Brandon said, casually following her onto the patio.

"Brandon, thanks again for all your help," she replied, smiling nervously at him.

"It was all my pleasure. Can I call you?" He whispered as he slowly walked past her, allowing his finger to slip down her bare back as he headed toward the waiting car.

She jumped at the power of his touch, "Yes, absolutely."

Brandon got into the car and Katherine waved before turning to go back inside. He caught a final glimpse of the back of that dress before Dr. Baker turned the car around and headed for home.

CHAPTER 19: SUNDAY MORNING

"How did it go last night?" Sharon asked, her smile filled with anticipation.

"Thank you, thank you, thank you! I had such a great time all thanks to you, my Fairy Godmother."

"Tell me everything!"

"First, your dress was the hit of the night. Holy crap, men couldn't keep their eyes off it. I felt like that dress has magic powers! Even the guys who parked the cars went wacky over that dress."

"That's what it was supposed to do. You know, that dress should come with a warning label! So, how was the new vet?"

"Brandon? He was fabulous!"

"Brandon? Ohhh, give me details," she giggled.

"First, the barn won six out of ten awards for the night. I was so shaky in your high heels and I had to walk up about 10 stairs every time to accept an award. Luckily Carl agreed to walk me up and down every time so I wouldn't break my neck. Then, Brandon asked me to dance and we danced through two slow songs and it got hot on the dance floor. It was so hot that when the music stopped, we didn't even notice."

"Yipeee! So, he must be single? I can see the change in your face. You look happier than I've seen you look in years."

"Yes, he's single. I am happy, thanks to you. The evening got cut short because Jimmy got drunk and I had to drive him home early but Brandon offered to come with me. It was amazing. We shared a brandy while Jimmy snored on the couch."

"Did you kiss him?"

"Brandon kissed me and then I kissed him back!"

"Tell me everything!"

Katherine shared all the juicy details and then said, "Oh Sharon it was enchanting and he's a great kisser. I've never felt that way before and I have you to thank for all of it."

"That's what I'm here for, to be your Fairy Godmother, slash, wing woman!! So, when are you going to see him again?"

"Geez, I don't know. When Bob called saying he was turning into the driveway, I was in such a rush to get him out the door that we never discussed it. He did ask if he could call me and I said yes, so I guess he'll call this week and we'll figure something out."

"You look and sound so happy. I'm doing the happy dance for you."

"Me too. Oh, I'm going to adjust the hem on your dress so it's ready for you and I'm going to have it dry cleaned this week. I'll ship everything back to you by Friday if that's OK with you? I can't thank you enough for everything you've done for me. It's a night I'll never forget."

"I couldn't love you more if you were my sister. I'll always want the best for you. Friday is fine or whenever you have time to send it back." Just then they could hear the familiar cry of the baby waking up in the other room, "Ooops, there goes the baby. Duty calls!"

"I'll let you go. I love you! Go kiss Pamela for me."

"Give Brandon a kiss for me. Talk to you later. Bye."

"Bye."

CHAPTER 20: THE DOMINATRIX

Katherine and Brandon tried unsuccessfully all week to get together for dinner but their schedules kept getting in the way. First it was an emergency call involving a sick cow. The next night, Katherine had a meeting at the Women's Shelter to discuss the upcoming fund raiser. After that, Brandon was up most of the night with a horse that colicked. They were able to share a few short phone calls, several voice mails and many one-sided text messages that Brandon sent, until he realized Katherine never turned her cell phone on unless she had to. The following Saturday morning, Katherine was preparing to attend a riding clinic at Vinton Farms with several of her clients.

"Jimmy, do me a favor. Would you dig in my purse, find my cell phone and turn it on for me?"

"Sure."

"I hope it's still charged. I haven't turned the damn thing on for weeks."

"Found it," Jimmy said triumphantly, as Katherine glanced over at him.

"Well done. Is there any juice left in it?"

"It is almost fully charged. I'll plug it into the charger while we drive and it should be fully charged by the time we get there. Just out of curiosity, why don't you use your cell phone?"

"I live where I work and I have a landline at the farm. The cell phone is a nuisance."

"If you never use this thing, why are we turning it on now?"

"Sarah knows I can be reached on the cell when I'm at a show, just in case something comes up at the farm. That's the only reason why," she smiled. "If I had my way, I wouldn't own the thing. Besides, I have no idea how to run it. I'm lucky if I can remember how to answer a call when it rings without hanging up on them," Jimmy laughed because he wouldn't be without his phone and was amazed that there was anyone on the planet who wasn't tied to their phone like an umbilical cord.

Ж

Once they arrived at Vinton Farms and unloaded, Brandon surprised Katherine by texting her. Her phone, which was now in her pocket, made a chirping noise that she didn't recognize.

"Jimmy, I think there's something wrong with my cell phone."

"Let me see," he replied, taking the phone from her hand. "Oh, you have a text message, looks like it's from Brandon," he showed it to her.

"I'm at the end of the aisle. Can u do lunch today?" She looked up and down the aisle until she spotted him at the very end. "Jimmy, can you text him back for me? I have no idea how to do this and if I have to figure it out, the show will be over before I get it done."

"No problem. What do you want me to say?"

"Will you say, YES, where and when?"

"Ok," Jimmy handily typed the text message and hit the send button. "It's done."

"Wow, you're fast," she discovered a newfound respect for Jimmy hearing her phone once again chirp.

"Here's your answer from Dr. Stafford."

"Meet me @ the clubhouse @ 12."

"Jimmy, can you answer for me?"

"What do you want to say?"

"How about, Meet you at noon?" She could feel her heart flutter with excitement as she looked down the aisle to see if he was still there. She spotted him. Brandon smiled and waved at her before heading back to work.

At 11:45, Katherine pulled Jimmy to the side and whispered, "Jimmy, do you mind if I duck out for lunch now?"

"Go have fun!"

"SHHHH," Katherine whispered. "We're supposed to meet at the club-house at noon and I should be back by 1:30. Can you take care of things while I'm gone?"

"You can count on me."

"Thanks, I knew I could. If you need me, I'll have my phone with me and I'm sure Brandon will know how to answer it." she released her pony tail and allowed her long wavy auburn hair to flow over her shoulders. Katherine arrived a few minutes early and entered the clubhouse, only to find Hadley Vinton alone in the room and it was clear he was anything but sober.

Katherine tried to say a quick hello and exit just as quickly but he yelled, "Katy, come in here, I have a question for you."

Afraid of what could happen, but feeling fairly certain she could out maneuver an overweight drunk if she had to, she entered the large room. *Hadley might be drunk, but he isn't crazy enough to make a pass at a barn owner during a busy clinic knowing anyone could walk in on him,* she reassured herself. "What did you want to ask me Hadley?"

He staggered across the room in her direction. Katherine slid a chair between them to keep him at bay as she tried to talk her way out of the encounter.

"Katy, we should be partners in business. Your skills on a horse and my business brains, we could go far," he said from the other side of the chair, clumsily trying to figure out a way to get around it. As he tried to circle the chair to get to her, he pushed the clubhouse door shut. When Katherine saw the door slam closed, she knew she was in trouble.

"Thanks for that vote of confidence. I'll certainly give it some thought. Look, I'm meeting someone for lunch and he'll be here any minute. We can talk about this another time," she managed to keep him at bay with the chair as she maneuvered around so she was close to the door. Certain that she was only two steps away from escape she turned to open the door.

Hadley grabbed her by her long hair and spun her around. He pushed her up against the wall next to the door. At little more than 120 pounds soaking wet, Katherine was no match for Hadley's rotund, nearly 300 pound bulk.

She knew she'd have to take a different tact if she was going to get out of this situation in one piece. "Hadley, we should talk about working together…but how's your wife going to feel about that?" She asked breathlessly, her body squeezed in a sandwich between Hadley and the wall.

"She doesn't care what I do, we have an open marriage." He held her by her hair and pressed his lips against hers in a sloppy, wet kiss. "Mmmm, you taste good," he proclaimed, his voice slurring from drink.

"Hadley, get off of me! You don't get to touch me unless and until we have an arrangement," Katherine commanded, her voice loud and angry. She was desperately trying to sound tough but inside, she was quaking with fear.

He backed away from her, with a surprised look on his face. Hadley took her by the wrist to lead her across the room toward the couch. *Don't let him get you to that couch, think, think of something... come on, think of something...*she thought frantically to herself. At the last minute, she thrust her foot in front of his, tangling their feet and sending them both sailing to the floor as the clubhouse door opened. It was Brandon. He looked shocked to see the pair land on the floor in front of him, Katherine scrambled to get away from Hadley who was trying to regain his bearings. The duo unaware that Brandon was standing in the doorway behind them.

Before Brandon could say a word, "Katy, come to me, we should join up. I want to join up with you," Hadley yelled to her from the floor. She grabbed the chair near the table in the clubhouse and got up from the slick tile floor as quickly as she could while backing away from him the whole time. Katherine noticed a dressage whip on the table and grabbed it. Unaware that Brandon was even in the room and without a moment's hesitation, she struck Hadley across the legs repeatedly with the three-foot-long whip, "Owww" he screamed, covering his face as she thrashed him with long, hard strokes.

"You son of a bitch, you shouldn't drink so much. What the hell is wrong with you?" She yelled at him, trying to catch her breath, from fear and from the sheer physicality of horse whipping him. Her strokes were slow, methodical and relentless. Brandon watched in amazement, the scene unfolding in front of him in a matter of seconds. There she stood in her tight black breeches and knee high black leather boots whipping a grown man as she chided him verbally like a dominatrix.

"Owww Katy, stop hitting me," he cried out, his voice slurring from his drunken stupor, one hand shielding his face and the other now shielding his crotch. Katherine bent over at the waist to catch her breath, resting her hands on her thighs, still holding the whip. "If you ever touch me again, I swear to God, there won't be enough left of you to bury. Do you hear me?" She growled.

"I hear you, I hear you," he pleaded. "I won't do it again."

Satisfied she'd made her point and well aware that she'd never turn her back on Hadley Vinton again, she slammed the dressage whip down on the table with the same level of defiance that a rapper drops the microphone to signify they'd given their all. Katherine started backing up, heading for the door and backed directly into the arms of Brandon. She screamed out, "shit!" as she spun around, her arms swinging before realizing it was him.

Brandon took her in his arms, "Kate, it's ok. It's just me," he stated calmly, trying to diffuse the situation. "Are you OK?" He asked without ever taking his eyes from Hadley.

"I'm fine," she said with conviction, even though her voice cracked as she spoke, still trying to catch her breath.

"Did Hadley hurt you?"

"No. I'm fine, but he's probably going to need some medical attention," she hissed.

"Stay here Kate," Brandon said, stepping away from Katherine, guiding her behind him as he addressed Hadley, "What the hell's going on in here?" He demanded, staring down at him as Hadley wriggled in pain. Hadley tried to get back on his feet but was unable to maneuver his mass effectively and it didn't help that every inch of his lower anatomy stung from the lashing.

"It's Ok Brandon...it's done now," Katherine said bending over, her hands on her thighs, still trying to catch her breath.

"No...thing. I just fell down and Katy was trying to help me up," he mumbled in his drunken stupor.

"Let's go. Please, let's just go," Katherine whispered to Brandon as she headed for the door. "Look, he's drunk and the only thing he'll remember tomorrow are the welts from the horse whipping I just gave him. It's my fault. I know what he is and I walked into the room. I just never thought he'd be this drunk, this early in the day. It was my mistake."

"Hadley, you're lucky I showed up when I did or she might have beaten you to a pulp," Brandon said with a small smile on his face. "Kate, wait a minute, he can't get off the floor on his own. I better help him up."

"Help him up...my ass. He can spend the rest of the day that way as far as I'm concerned!" Brandon smiled, as they left the room with Hadley still lying on his back moaning.

The pair headed for the parking lot, Katherine was both angry and embarrassed. "Kate, what happened back there?"

She stopped in her tracks, their eyes met and Brandon could see she was still shaking from the adrenaline in her system. "Hadley's a drunk and I made the mistake of walking into the room before I realized he was in there. It was my own fault, I should have learned my lesson the last time."

"Wait a minute, Hadley's done this to you before?" Brandon voice filled with outrage. "Kate, I'm calling the police," he pulled his cell phone out of his pocket.

"No, it wasn't Hadley. Never mind...I can't report this..." She said, putting her hand over his phone to stop him.

"What do you mean you can't report this? He assaulted you. You have every right to call the police and have him arrested."

She took a deep breath before calmly saying, "Sheriff Mac Cameron is my good friend and if he finds out Hadley tried to hurt me, Hadley will lose Vinton Farms and his freedom. Hadley made a pass at me, it got a bit hairy before you walked in. I took care of it, Hadley is never going to do that to me again and it's over."

"Are you sure you don't want me to call the police?"

"I'm sure," she insisted.

"Do you want me to go back in there and at least beat him up?" Brandon smiled, hoping to break the tension.

Katherine found his offer both sweet and funny, "You're too late. I just served him justice with that dressage whip, but I appreciate the offer! Just out of curiosity, how long were you standing there?"

Brandon smiled as he stroked her cheek tenderly, "I walked in around the time you started kicking his ass. *Katherine the Great*, you're pretty impressive in your black boots and dressage whip. You looked like a dominatrix. More importantly, you sounded like one!"

"I have to give props to those women, whipping men while yelling at them is really hard work. I'm exhausted!" she mused. "By the way, dairy-farmer boy, how would you know what a dominatrix sounds like?"

"I read a lot! This is the second time I thought I needed to step in to help you and both times you proved me wrong," he hugged her warmly. Brandon had never been so turned on in his life.

"If I have my way, you'll never have to save my bacon. I'd like to think I can take care of myself."

"If you ever do need me, I'm there. I'm glad you weren't hurt. However, it was pretty clear, you're one bad ass. I sure don't ever want to be on your bad side. You definitely deserve the title, *Katherine the Great* after what I just witnessed." Brandon said with pride in his voice and desire in his heart.

"Shoot, I was going for smart and sexy, or tall and willowy, but I guess I'll have to settle for being a bad ass. I warned you that I'm not very good dating material. Just for the record, beating someone's ass works up an appetite, so where are we going for lunch?"

CHAPTER 21: WEDNESDAY NIGHT

"Hi Sharon, how's everyone?"

"They're all fine. Roger's enjoying the new job promotion. So far, he isn't working extra hours so we're thrilled about that, and the extra money is always welcome. Having babies is expensive!"

"Speaking of babies, how's the baby?"

"Pamela is perfect. She's just perfect. So, what's going on with you? Have you seen Brandon?"

"Actually, we met for lunch at the riding clinic at Hadley Vinton's place over the weekend. Brandon was the vet on call and I had clients there. He invited me out to lunch, so we snuck away for an hour or so."

"Did you make out?"

"NO. We ate lunch and talked."

"Sounds boring if you ask me."

"It was anything but!"

"What do you mean?" Katherine relayed the events in the clubhouse to Sharon.

"Holy crap, were you OK?"

"Yea, but I don't think Hadley was. I'm thinking he's still carrying welts on his legs and lower body. I came pretty close to castrating that son of a bitch. That's one horse whipping he won't soon forget. God, he smelled of liquor and tried to force himself on me and the whole thing reminded me...well, I just snapped and went off on him," she said shaking her head.

"Oh, shit! I'm sorry you had to go through that...although, that might not be such a bad thing, you know?"

"What?"

"It made me think that you've been haunted by what happened six years ago, even though you shouldn't be. I'm just glad to see that this time, instead of feeling helpless you tore into the guy like a pole cat. I'd say that's a good thing. By the way, what did Brandon think or did he know?"

"He didn't see Hadley pin me or grope me. He came in when I was getting off the floor and started horse whipping the SOB. When it was over, Brandon offered to go back and beat him up which I thought was sweet."

"That was sweet."

"He was insistent that we should call the police. You know I can't call the police and risk them finding out about my past but Brandon didn't know so he was trying to be helpful. He called me a bad ass. He was really kind and supportive though."

"It's good that Brandon knows you can take care of yourself and it's nice that he knows you're a bad ass. I guess if you have to be known for something, that's better than being known as a helpless damsel in distress any day!"

Katherine snorted with laughter, "I doubt Brandon Stafford will ever think of me as a helpless damsel in distress now. Not after he watched me horse whip a 300 pound man into submission. He told me I looked and sounded like a dominatrix, hardly the stuff that helpless damsels are made of."

"So, when are you going to see each other again?"

"I don't know! We never seem to get to that part of the conversation when we're together. I think he's coming out to the barn next Friday to work on a horse but we'll probably speak on the phone before then."

"Why can't you call him and schedule something this week?"

"Between his wacky hours and mine, getting together during the week is pretty tough. Besides, until he gets an assistant or someone else to cover the emergency calls, even when we do schedule time together, that damned cell phone of his goes off and he has to leave. That's another reason why I hate cell phones!"

"You know, you can text him throughout the day. That's what Roger and I do. It's very romantic."

"No. YOU could text him…I can barely answer a call on that damned thing, let alone figure out how to text on it!"

"Ok, skip the texting idea, but keep me updated on how it's going with Brandon!"

"Will do Fairy Godmother. Be sure to give Roger and that baby a kiss for me too."

"Love ya Kate, I'll talk to you next week."

"Love you more, bye."

CHAPTER 22: FRIDAY

The big horse show was one day away. The weather called for thunderstorms but fortunately, the show and stabling were all indoors making the weather a non-issue for the team. The staff was busy packing trailers and checking off lists of last-minute items in preparation for their departure later that afternoon.

"Morning Jimmy. Have you checked the schedule for today?" Katherine asked as she entered the barn at 8:00 am.

"Yea, you have Brandy on the books to work and two lessons this morning. Dr. Stafford is coming out at 1:00 to give Beau his last shot and remove the stitches. The rest of the day is packing for the show. I think everyone's scheduled to leave around 4:00 pm so they can get the horses settled before checking into their hotels for the night."

"Great! I'm looking forward to seeing Brandon. Do you know if Denise is planning on being here when he comes? You and I are going to be tied up prepping for the show, but I want to make sure someone is there to help him with Beau."

"Denise told me yesterday she was planning on being here."

"I would rather you or I handle Beau, just in case, but he's Denise's horse and she needs to learn how to do these things so, I'll leave it up to her."

Ӝ

Between her schedule and the hustle and bustle of the staff preparing for the show, the morning went by quickly. Katherine ate lunch at home before returning to the barn at 1:10 pm, carrying a loaf of banana bread that she'd baked for Brandon the night before. There were some serious storm clouds forming to the south as she exited her truck. Brandon's truck was already in front of the barn. As she entered the building, she could hear Brandon in the aisle with Denise. Katherine ducked into her office, first to drop off the loaf of banana bread and then to take a quick peek at herself in the mirror before heading down the aisle to say hello.

"Steady son, whoa," she heard Brandon's calm but firm voice, followed by the all too familiar sound of an impatient horse pawing at the concrete floor. Turning the corner, she could see Beau in the aisle using his front hoof to strike out at Brandon. Normally a sweet animal, Beau had been poked and prodded for several days. Denise was afraid to ride him until he was completely healed so he was full of pent up energy and fed up with people. No one could blame him for getting cranky. However, Katherine also knew this could be a dangerous situation for both Brandon and Denise. 1200 pounds of angry, impatient horse could do a lot of damage to any handler.

"Hi Brandon. Hey Denise," Katherine approached both people in the aisle and hugged each of them, breaking the tension that was all too apparent. She kept a watchful eye on Beau at all times. Brandon hugged her a bit firmer and longer than one might normally hug a client. The couple locked eyes for just a moment, happy to see each other. Brandon knew that Katherine was desperate to keep their private life, private so he kept things very professional.

"Hi Katherine it's good to see you." When alone, he called her Kate but when he was there in a professional capacity, he chose to call her Katherine. He didn't understand why Katherine was so jumpy about people knowing she had a personal life, but Brandon respected her concerns just the same.

"Hi Katherine," Denise answered, her voice a bit shaky.

"So, how's it going with Beau?"

"My Beau seems upset today. He doesn't want to stand still for Dr. Stafford and he's been pawing and striking. It's making me nervous." As she spoke, there was a rumble of thunder outside as the storm approached.

"Denise, I'm sure it's just the thunder getting Beau upset. Let me give you a hand before we get Dr. Stafford hurt," Katherine offered. The look on Denise's face was one of great relief.

"Thanks Katherine. I'm sure you're right, it's probably the thunder and I wouldn't mind some help," Denise replied nervously. Brandon made eye contact with Katherine, the look of relief also visible on his face.

"Denise, I'll take the lead line."

"No, that's alright, Beau's my horse and I should hold the lead line for Dr. Stafford."

"Are you sure you feel up to the task?"

"Sure, I'll be fine."

"Ok then, Brandon, I'm going to pick up his hind hoof to help out."

"His hind hoof?" Denise asked.

"Yep, horses are like a four-legged table, with one leg off the ground, he won't be striking at Dr. Stafford anymore. Beau's smart enough to know that a two-legged table can't stay upright. I'd hold up a front hoof but then I'd get in your way, so, I'll lift a hind and that should solve the problem. Denise, your job is to control Beau's head because wherever that's pointed, the rest of him will follow. Control the head and you control the horse. For now, keep his head pointed away from Dr. Stafford. We don't want him to get bit."

Denise laughed nervously, "Beau would never bite Dr. Stafford."

"I meant Dr. Stafford might bite Beau." The trio laughed, essentially breaking the tension. Katherine stood on the right side of the horse and raised his rear hoof, cradling it in her right hand, rocking it just enough to keep the horse's focus on what she was doing, rather than on what Brandon was doing.

"Thanks Katherine. I'll finish up as quickly as I can. I only have a few more stitches to pull and then we're done," Brandon said as he continued to work.

"No worries, do what you need to do. I'm not going anywhere."

A few moments later, Brandon announced, "I'm almost finished

Katherine." Suddenly, there was a loud crack of thunder and Jennifer's nine-year-old new student, Tommy Klassen raced into the barn from behind the trio.

"Holy smokes, did you hear that thunder?" he screamed as he ran down the aisle in his cowboy boots toward the team.

"No running in the barn," Katherine called out to Tommy. "Head's up," she shouted to Brandon and Denise as Tommy ran by both of them, tripping over Brandon's metal tool box which made a huge banging noise, spooking Beau who tried to bolt forward to escape.

Tommy stopped running when he saw Jennifer step out of the tack room into his path. Katherine refused to put down the rear leg until she was sure everyone was safe, no matter how much Beau was bent on escape. "Whoa son," Katherine said calmly as she raised his hoof even higher to keep him off balance and less likely to try and take a step forward, "Brandon, he's going to blow. Let me know when you're both clear," she called out calmly, as Beau tried to head down the aisle on three legs with Katherine in tow, still on her feet, refusing to let go. Katherine was very fond of Denise but when it came to diffusing a frightened horse, Denise had no experience so it was clear Beau was going to blow and it was going to happen soon.

Jennifer grabbed Tommy and pulled him into the safety of the tack room seconds before all hell broke loose in the aisle. "I've got Tommy," Jennifer called out to Katherine. Jimmy was across the indoor and heard the commotion. He hurried toward the aisle, but was too late.

"We're clear," Brandon yelled stepping quickly out of the line of fire, moving his tool kit at the same time. Denise extended her left arm to push Beau's head straight in order to keep her feet out of the line of fire. She hadn't worked around many horses in her life and didn't realize that by pointing Beau's nose straight ahead she inadvertently presented him with the perfect escape route. Without realizing it, she'd just put Katherine's life in jeopardy.

"Whoa...son" Brandon said, suddenly realizing what Denise was unknowingly doing. He tried to grab for the horse's halter to contain the frightened animal, but it was too late. Just as Katherine began to lower the back leg, giving up her leverage, putting herself in the most vulnerable position, Beau saw that he now had a clear escape route in front of him. In an attempt to flee, the frightened animal kicked his rear leg out mightily, one time, sending Katherine flying into the wall like a rag doll as he took off at a trot down the aisle with Denise racing to keep up at the end of the lead line. Fortunately, Beau didn't kick Katherine, he kicked out to shake her off, but a kick with 1200 pounds of force behind it against her 120 pounds was tantamount to brushing away a fly with a shotgun. The entire incident was over in less than 10 seconds.

Katherine's back and head made a frighteningly loud thud as they crashed into the solid barn wall. She gasped loudly, her body slowly slipping its way down toward the concrete floor where she sat against the stall wall motionless, her eyes closed.

Brandon rushed down the aisle to check on her but as Brandon approached her body slowly collapsed sideways and came to rest on the concrete aisle.

"Tommy, don't you move," Jennifer commanded before racing over to find Katherine motionless, blood streaming down her face from a thin cut on her hairline.

The sound of the rain echoed against the metal roof as the storm rolled in. Brandon knelt down next to Katherine, "Kate. Kate, can you hear me?" His voice was calm but inside he was terrified. He turned to see Jennifer standing there, "Call 911." Jimmy approached in time to see Brandon gently scoop Katherine up in his arms, cradling her bleeding head against his chest, trying not to move her spine any more than he had to.

"She'll fire me if I call 911 Brandon," Jennifer said nervously.

"Jennifer, make the call," Brandon shouted as he was already well on his way down the long aisle heading for Katherine's office...

HERE IS AN EXCERPT FROM BOOK 2,

FOX RIDGE LOVERS OR LIARS

Brandon carefully laid Katherine on the leather couch in her office, Jimmy followed close behind. The staff and boarders crowded around the office door. Only then did he realize she had a cut on her right hand probably from the nails on the horse's shoe.

"Jimmy, can you get me some ice and clean, wet towels?" Brandon asked with clear focus, kneeling down next to Katherine as she lay motionless on the couch.

Soon, the ice and towels materialized. "Kate, can you hear me?" He asked quietly, not wanting to startle her, still getting no response. He was worried, both by the fact that she was unresponsive and by the amount of blood she was losing. He knew that head wounds were notorious for bleeding heavily but it still worried him. Brandon soon dropped the first blood stained towel on the floor next to him and wrapped ice in one of the remaining towels, placing it over the wound to keep the swelling down. "Jimmy, would you get my bag and more clean towels?"

"I'll get them."

"Kate... Kate, can you hear me?" Brandon whispered, still getting no response.

Ж

Jennifer completed her call to 911 and realized that Mrs. Klassen had just arrived to pick up her son Tommy.

"Jennifer, what's all the commotion?"

"Tommy caused a serious accident."

"What, my Tommy? Where is he?"

"In the tack room, or at least he better be because that's where I told him to stay," she stated with an air of clear, unapologetic threat in her voice.

Mrs. Klassen rushed down the aisle and found Tommy standing in the tack room crying. "Sugga', what happened?"

"Jennifer yelled at me. I didn't do anything. They're mean to me here mommy." Just then, Carl entered the tack room. He'd parked at the back of the barn to avoid getting wet.

"What's up?" he asked innocently, noticing Jennifer was involved in what appeared to be a heated discussion with Mrs. Klassen.

"Katherine got hurt holding a horse for Dr. Stafford when Tommy spooked the horse."

"Don't blame my Tommy for your negligence. I have a good mind to sue you people for endangering my son."

"Where is she?"

"Dr. Stafford carried her into her office and the paramedics are on the way."

"Holy shit!"

"Don't you cuss in front of my child! Oh, you poor darlin'," Mrs. Klassen said hugging her son tightly. "Let me take you home." As the pair left the tack room, Jennifer approached.

"Mrs. Klassen, didn't you go over the barn rules with Tommy?"

"What barn rules?"

"The ones I gave you last week!"

"It's your job to teach, not mine. Tommy's clearly upset by the way you spoke to him today. We're leaving. Come on Tommy, let's stop and get you some ice cream on the way home."

Jennifer was dumfounded by Mrs. Klassen's cavalier attitude and she couldn't help but notice the smile on Tommy's face as he walked by her. Prayer, Jennifer decided was the only answer. So she prayed her version of the serenity prayer: *God, give me five minutes alone with this spoiled little boy. I just want to whoop his backside once or twice to get his attention. If you can't give me five minutes alone with that brat, can you at least find a way to kick his momma's backside? There's no question, the rotten apple didn't fall far from the tree at the Klassen house... In the name of Jesus, Amen.* Even as Jennifer was thinking of what she wanted to do to Tommy and his mother, she knew God was not likely to answer that particular prayer.

As Mrs. Klassen approached Katherine's office, she could hear Carl, "Jimmy, what the hell happened to Katherine? Is she OK?"

"She was knocked out when Beau spooked and she hasn't come to yet. I'm worried." Just then, Mrs. Klassen tried to get to the exit through the crowd with her son. She could see Katherine lying motionless on the couch, the blood stained towel on the floor and Dr. Stafford leaning over her.

"Tommy, we need to leave before these people get you hurt." Carl overheard her comment and lit into her verbally before Jennifer interceded and calmed him down. It was obvious that Mrs. Klassen had never been spoken to in such a harsh manner in her entire life and she was quite shook-up.

Mrs. Klassen shuffled Tommy out the door quickly. She was embarrassed and mad on a level that only polite Southern women can attain. That kind of mad ultimately and predictably explodes all over its victims it just takes polite Southern women a minute to decide how they're going to destroy their prey. "Carl, knock it off!" Jennifer insisted in a hushed but firm tone as she held Carl back.

"That stupid woman could be responsible for killing Katherine because she has no control over her dumb ass son!" Carl demanded in an irate, hushed tone.

"Carl, there are customers here, shut up. Besides, it's not Tommy's fault. It's mine."

"What are you talking about?"

The pair now speaking in agitated whispers. "Katherine has been after me for weeks to rein Tommy in. She told me several times how dangerous his behavior in the barn has been. I thought she was being anal and he was just being a normal kid. I was wrong and now, Katherine could die and if that happens, it'll be my fault."

Just then, the pair was interrupted when they heard Jimmy ask Brandon, "Is Katherine going to be alright?" …

Will Katherine be alright?

Will we find out the secret that has controlled Katherine's life since leaving New York?

What will happen with the job offer in Canada?

If you enjoyed this book, I'd like to ask you to leave an online review so you can help others enjoy it as well.

Order Book 1 in the Fox Ridge Series
Fox Ridge
The Secret

Order Book 2 in the Fox Ridge Series
Fox Ridge Lovers or Liars

Order Book 3 in the Fox Ridge Series
Fox Ridge Friend or Foe

Order Book 4 in the Fox Ridge Series
Fox Ridge
The Phoenix

Order Book 5 in the Fox Ridge Series
Fox Ridge
Gifts for the Holidays

OTHER TITLES FROM BONNIE

For more information about Bonnie's other books, click on any of the titles below or visit:
http://whitehallpr.com/fr.html

Special Reports for Authors and Non-Profits

So, You Want to Publish Your First book
How to Promote Your Book
Selling your Work to Magazines
Writing Press Releases That Work
Your Event Planning Report
Non-Profits, How to Attract More Individual Donors
Non-Profits, How to Attract More Business Sponsors
Making Profits for Your Non-Profit

Books for Animal Lovers

The Great Horse Breeds of the World
Pet Treat Cookbook
Horse Tales for the Soul, full set of 7 books

Horse Tales for the Soul, Vol 1
Horse Tales for the Soul, Vol 1 Kindle
Horse Tales for the Soul, Vol 2
Horse Tales for the Soul, Vol 2 Kindle
Horse Tales for the Soul, Vol 3
Horse Tales for the Soul, Vol 3 Kindle
Horse Tales for the Soul, Vol 4
Horse Tales for the Soul, Vol 4 Kindle
Horse Tales for the Soul, Vol 5
Horse Tales for the Soul, Vol 5 Kindle
Horse Tales for the Soul, Vol 6
Horse Tales for the Soul, Vol 6 Kindle
Horse Tales for the Soul, Vol 7
Horse Tales for the Soul, Vol 7 Kindle
Dog Tales for the Soul
Dog Tales for the Funny Bone
Horse Tales for the Funny Bone
A Parent's Guide To Buying That First Horse
Debugging Your Horse
Happy Endings, Vol 1
Happy Endings, Vol 2

94467518R00082

Made in the USA
Middletown, DE
20 October 2018